ELIJAH WOLFE

SANDI LYNN

SANDI LYNN ROMANCE, LLC

ELIJAH WOLFE

New York Times, USA Today & Wall Street Journal
Bestselling Author
Sandi Lynn

Elijah Wolfe

Cover Photo by Wander Aguiar
Model: Gil S.

❀ Created with Vellum

MISSION STATEMENT

Sandi Lynn Romance

*Providing readers with romance novels that will whisk them away
to another world and from the daily grind of life – one book at a time.*

CHAPTER 1

𝒶 spen
"There's something I need to talk to you about," Ron whispered in my ear as he walked up to me and placed his hand on my shoulder.

"Sure." I smiled.

I told my cousin, Carrie, that I'd talk to her later and followed Ron outside to the patio where it was quiet.

"What's up, babe? Did you get a chance to try my Aunt Patti's spinach dip?"

"Aspen, I didn't call you out here to talk about your Aunt Patti's spinach dip."

"Okay. What do you want to talk about?"

He placed his hands in his pants pockets, took in a deep breath, and turned away from me for a moment."

"Ron, what's going on?"

"I'm breaking up with you," he blurted out.

"What? That isn't funny, Ron."

"It's not meant to be funny, Aspen." He turned around and faced me. "I don't want to be with you anymore."

As I heard the words escape his lips, a sickness formed in the pit of my belly and my heart started racing.

"What? Why?" I asked in shock. "We've been together for over a year. What changed?"

"I did, and I finally came to realize some things."

"Is there another woman?"

"No." He shook his head.

He was lying, and I knew it. I knew every single time he lied to me. Suddenly, an anger rose up inside. A rage so fierce I couldn't control it.

"Bullshit!" I yelled. "You're lying. You know how I know you're lying? That little vein between your eyes always pulsates.

I took off my shoe and threw it. He put his arms up and shielded his face as my shoe hit him.

"What is going on out here?" My sister, Geneva, asked as she slid the patio door open.

"You son of a bitch." I jammed my finger into his chest as he walked backwards and tripped inside the door. "How long? How long have you been seeing her behind my back?"

"It doesn't matter, Aspen. You need to calm the fuck down!"

"I gave you a year of my life. I gave you my heart, and this is how you treat me? By cheating and breaking up with me at my father's funeral!" I shouted.

Everyone stopped their conversations, and all eyes were on us. He continued walking backwards through the living room as my finger jammed into his chest.

"I'm sorry. I couldn't put it off any longer."

"You are a worthless piece of shit, Ronald Needham. Get the hell out of my house!" I shouted while I took off my other shoe and threw it at him as he ran out the door. I swallowed hard as I stood there in the silent room where my family and friends gathered to pay their respects to my father. "I apologize. If you'll excuse me, I'm going up to my room for a while. Please, make yourselves another plate of food. There's plenty in the kitchen." I graciously smiled as I slowly walked up the stairs.

The moment I shut the door, I face planted myself onto the bed. Crying over it wasn't an option for me. I never cried. The last time I cried was when I was a child. I didn't even cry at my own father's funeral.

"Sweetheart?" I heard my mother's voice as she opened the door, stepped inside and sat on the edge of the bed. "Are you okay?"

"Do I look like I'm okay, Mom?"

She softly rubbed my back, and I wanted to scream at her to stop.

"I didn't like him. The nerve of him doing this to you at your father's funeral."

"You're not helping." My brows furrowed.

"I'm sorry, Aspen. I know it hurts now, but in time you'll see this as a blessing in disguise. Anyway, you can't sit up here and sulk until all the guests have left. So come on." She slapped me on the butt.

I sighed as I sat up and went to face the embarrassment of earlier events. Sympathetic smiles greeted me as I walked down the stairs.

"Are you okay?" Geneva hooked her arm around me as we walked into the kitchen.

"How could he do this to me? And especially today of all days?"

"He's an asshole. Plain and simple. You can do so much better."

As soon as the last of the guests left, I grabbed an open bottle of wine and took it to the couch. Bringing my knees up to my chest, I began to guzzle it.

"Whoa, slow down there, killer," my brother-in-law Lucas said as he grabbed the bottle from me and poured some wine into a glass. "Here."

"Thanks. He was supposed to be here for me during this time, not break up with me."

Lucas sighed as he sat down and hooked his arm around me.

"I know, Aspen, but the guy is a jerk. You can do much better than him."

"Why do I always fall for the jerks?" I laid my head on his shoulder.

"Maybe because you know they'll eventually leave."

"Oh. Are you shrinking me now?" I smiled.

"No. But I can if you want me to."

3

"Not really in the mood."

"Okay." He kissed the side of my head. "I'm going upstairs to check my emails. If you want to talk just let me know."

As soon as he got up and left, my mother and her husband, Raphael, walked into the room.

"Darling, we have to go. Our flight leaves in three hours."

"I thought you weren't leaving until tomorrow."

"Change of plans. We need to get back to L.A. Raphael has a showing he needs to get ready for."

"Okay. Call me when you get back." I got up from the couch and hugged her.

"I will. Are you going to be okay?"

"I'm fine, Mom. Bye, Raphael."

"Goodbye, darling. It was a nice service." He hugged me tight.

I grabbed the bottle of wine off the coffee table, turned on some music, and began to dance around the living room.

"Oh hey, a dance party!" Geneva smiled as she joined me.

Dancing was always my escape. It was my stress reliever. Some people took baths, did yoga, or went for walks. But not me. I danced it all away.

CHAPTER 2

*E*lijah

"We the jury find the defendant not guilty."

"Yes." I silently spoke and turned to my client who let out a sigh of relief. "Congratulations, Bob." I grinned as I lightly hugged him.

"Thank you, Elijah. This wouldn't have been possible without you."

I closed up my briefcase, grabbed it from the table, and walked out of the courtroom. Pulling my phone from my pocket, I noticed I had three missed calls from Vi, a text message from my brother, Nathan, and a voice message from Vi.

"Elijah, we need to talk."

I sighed as I rolled my eyes and opened the text message from Nathan.

"Hey, bro. I'm taking off for Paris in a few. I'll meet you and Mason in Hawaii in a few days. Can't wait for this vacation. Long overdue. See you soon."

I smile as I type my reply.

"Have a safe flight. Beaches, sun and beautiful women, here we come."

I walked back to the firm and as I was heading towards my office, my secretary, Marie, jumped up from her chair.

"Elijah, I thought I should warn you that Vi is waiting for you in your office."

"Shit. How long has she been here?"

"An hour."

"Thanks for the warning, Marie."

I opened my office door and stepped inside.

"Since you can't bother to call me back, I decided I would sit here and wait for you."

I could tell her tone was an angry one, but I wouldn't let her ruin my good mood.

"Vi, I was in court. I told you this morning I wouldn't be around today."

"Too bad. I got a call earlier from Patsy. She told me she saw you two days ago having dinner with some brunette who looked like a prostitute. It was the same night you canceled our date because you had too much work to do for an upcoming case. I want an explanation now, Elijah," she demanded in the harsh tone that I couldn't stand anymore.

Shit. I set my briefcase down and leaned against my desk, placing my hands in my pockets as I stared at her.

"She was a client. End of discussion."

"You're a liar!" she voiced rather loudly.

"Vi, I don't have time for this. Not today and not tomorrow. You do not question what I do. Understand me?" I spoke in an authoritative tone.

"So you're seeing other women? I assumed we were exclusive."

"Did I ever say we were exclusive? You know what they say about people who assume." I took a seat behind my desk.

"We've been seeing each other for two months, Elijah. Two fucking months, and I have never once looked at another man. I even overlooked the fact that you wouldn't let me go to Hawaii with you."

"That's a trip for me and my brothers. No women allowed."

"Yeah, so you can fuck as many women as you want. God, you're just a pathetic lying asshole. My friends warned me about you, and I should have listened."

"Perhaps you should have. Whatever you thought we had is over. I have work to do so you need to leave."

"I don't understand how you even live with yourself. Whatever stuff you left at my place, I'm burning. Good riddance, bastard." She stormed out of my office.

A moment later, Marie walked in.

"And another one bites the dust." She smiled.

I leaned back in my chair and sighed.

"Block her number and let security know she's not allowed in the building."

"On it. Congratulations on winning the case."

"Thanks. I knew the jury would swing in our favor." I smiled.

"Don't forget that Harry's going away party is at Rudy's at seven."

"I haven't forgotten. Have we found his replacement yet?"

"No. Your mother said she'll start scheduling interviews when you get back from Hawaii because she wants you to sit in on them like always. In the meantime, Roger is taking his open cases."

❧

"*M*an, I need this vacation so bad," my brother Mason said as we sipped our drinks in first class. "So, I heard you gave Vi the boot." He smiled.

"And where did you hear that from?" I arched my brow.

"Allison said that Marie told her."

"I keep forgetting you two work together at the fire station. She was waiting for me in my office when I got back from court. Apparently, a friend of hers saw me and Danielle out to dinner the same night I canceled my date with her. She demanded answers." I rolled my eyes.

"Good call. If a woman demanded answers from me, I'd get rid of her too. There's nothing more annoying than a woman trying to control your life. It's bad enough Mom still tries to do it."

"Here's to meeting up with Nathan, relaxing, and fucking beautiful

7

women we won't have to worry about seeing again." I smirked as I held up my glass.

"Touché, bro. Touché."

We landed in Honolulu and found Nathan in baggage claim.

"It's about time you two douchebags got here." He smiled as he hugged us.

"How was Paris?" I asked.

"Beautiful as always. Great weather and great sex."

"You were only there three days, and you scored?" Mason asked.

"The French women can't resist me and my charm." A smirk crossed his lips.

"Well, let's hope we have the same luck here. Watch out Honolulu, the Wolfe brothers have arrived," I spoke as the three of us high-five each other.

CHAPTER 3

*A*spen

My father's dying wish was to have his ashes scattered over the waters in Hawaii. Honolulu to be exact. It was his home away from home. He vacationed there every year for three weeks and even considered moving before he became ill.

I held the urn tightly against my chest as we sailed across the blue waters of the Pacific. Geneva, Lucas, and I rented a boat to fulfill our father's wish.

"This looks like a good spot," Geneva spoke. "Are you ready?"

"Yeah. I think so."

The light wind swept across me as I removed the lid. Geneva placed her hands on mine as we walked around the boat and scattered his ashes over the water.

"Goodbye, Dad."

"May you rest in eternal peace, Dad," Geneva spoke.

"I miss him already," I said as we stared out into the ocean.

"I do too," Geneva spoke as she wiped her eye and then hooked her arm around me.

*J*t was our last night in Hawaii, so Geneva and Lucas went to do some last-minute sightseeing while I went down to the hotel bar.

"Are you sure you don't want to come with us?" she asked.

"You two go and don't worry about me. I just want to sit outside at the bar and have a few drinks."

"You mean you want to be alone for a while," Geneva said.

"Yeah." I gave her a soft smile.

"Okay. I get it. Just don't drown your sorrows too much. We have an early flight to catch."

"I know. Go have some fun. I have a date with some vodka." I grinned.

I went upstairs to my room, changed into a short white sundress with spaghetti straps, and headed down to the bar. Luckily, there was a seat available.

"Aloha. What can I get you?" The cute bartender smiled as he set a napkin down in front of me.

"A cosmopolitan please."

"One cosmopolitan coming right up."

I glanced around at my surroundings. Night had fallen, and the party was just beginning. People gathered at the small tables that filled the space. Fire pits were lit all around, and tiki torches were strategically placed. Laughter and conversation surrounded me. Everyone was having a good time while I sat on the stool mourning my father and thinking about how much I hated Ron.

"Here you go. Can I get you anything else?" The bartender asked.

"Another one when this is gone." I smiled.

"I'll keep an eye on you." He winked.

I finished my drink and signaled the bartender.

"Another?"

"Please. Could you make sure nobody sits here? I need to use the ladies' room."

"Will do."

After using the bathroom, I pulled my phone from my purse,

opened the door, and ran smack dab into someone as he was walking out of the men's room.

"Oh, my gosh. I'm sorry," I spoke as I looked up and nearly stopped breathing.

"I'm not." The hot as hell guy standing in front of me spoke with a smile.

I could feel the heat in my cheeks rise as I bit down on my bottom lip.

"I was looking down at my phone and I didn't see you."

"Like I said, I'm not sorry."

"Okay. Well, enjoy your evening," I nervously spoke as I high-tailed it back to my stool at the bar.

Letting out a deep breath, I picked up my drink and took a large sip. A little over six feet tall, short brown hair, dreamy chocolate brown eyes, a masculine jawline and my most favorite turn on: a perfect five o'clock shadow. Shit, he was sexy as sin and I'd never forget the smell of his cologne that radiated from him. It was crisp yet refined with a hint of citrus and wood. My heart was still racing. Maybe it was from the alcohol. No, it definitely was that sexy man I bumped into.

"If you're truly sorry for bumping into me, then you'll let me buy you a drink," I heard a low familiar voice from behind.

Oh, my God. It was him.

"Excuse me, friend, if you give up your stool, your next three drinks are on me," he spoke to the older gentleman sitting next to me.

"Sure. Take it."

The sexy man held up his finger, and the bartender walked over.

"The next three drinks for my friend here are on my tab," he said.

"Sure thing, man."

"And also, whatever drink this beautiful woman has had and will have are also on my tab."

"Really, you don't have to do that." I smiled.

"I know I don't. I want to." A sly smile crossed his lips.

He took a seat on the stool and ordered himself a scotch.

"Are you here alone?" he asked.

"At this bar, yes. In Hawaii, no. I'm here with my sister and her husband. We scattered my father's ashes in the Pacific."

"I'm sorry for your loss." He placed his hand on my knee, and I thought I would lose all control.

"Thank you." I blushed. "How about you?"

"I'm here with my two younger brothers."

"How much younger? You're pretty young yourself." I smiled.

"I'm thirty-two, Nathan is thirty, and Mason is twenty-eight. I'd say you're what? Twenty-five." He grinned.

"Thank you. But add five years."

"You don't look a day over twenty-five." He winked. "My name is Elijah." He held out his hand.

"Aspen." The moment our hands touched, it felt like a lightning bolt shot through me.

"It's nice to meet you, Aspen."

I quickly removed my hand from his and picked up my drink.

"It's nice to meet you too, Elijah. Isn't it kind of weird we're both here with our siblings?" I asked like an idiot.

"Since you put it that way, yes." He grinned. "But to be honest, I'm surprised your boyfriend back home didn't come with you for support during this difficult time."

"Ha." I laughed. "My boyfriend, now ex-boyfriend, broke up with me at my father's funeral. So that would make me single." I took a sip of my drink. "Very single."

"Wow. He sounds like a complete douchebag."

"He is." I set my glass down.

"Can I let you in on a little secret?"

"Sure."

He leaned in until his lips were mere inches from my ear.

"I think you're a very sexy and beautiful woman and your ex is a complete idiot for letting you go," he whispered.

The warmth of his breath on my skin made me tremble. He wanted sex, and he wanted it bad. As for me, my lady parts couldn't control themselves and I could feel the wetness in my panties. I was vulnerable, and I knew it. Perhaps he knew it too. He was one hell of a sexy guy, and the only thing floating around in my dirty little mind was his perfect body on top of mine. I had a couple one-night stands in my lifetime. No big deal. This was Hawaii and what happened in Hawaii would stay in Hawaii. I'd never see him again so there would be no embarrassment. And one day, when I'd tell the story of how I took a trip and scattered my father's ashes in the Pacific, the memory of this sexy man and our one-night affair would come to mind.

"Thank you, Elijah. You want to have sex with me, don't you?"

"You're very observant, Aspen." He smirked.

"Are you sharing a room with your brothers?"

"No. We each have our own rooms."

"Well, I'm sharing a suite with my sister. So if we're going to do this, we have to go to your room."

He got up from his stool with a smile on his face and held out his arm. Hooking mine around his, we headed out of the bar and to the elevator.

CHAPTER 4

Elijah

She was sexy as hell. All five feet six inches of her. The way her white dressed hugged her hourglass figure had me hard from the moment I saw her. Or maybe it was the way her long wavy blonde hair flowed over her shoulders, or her piercing baby blue eyes. She was everything wrapped up in a neat little package ready to be opened.

The moment we stepped into the elevator and the doors shut, I couldn't control myself. Grabbing her wrists, I smashed my mouth into hers as I pressed her against the wall with her arms over her head. I introduced my tongue to hers and they tangled like nobody's business. The elevator dinged, alerting me it had stopped on my floor. The doors opened, but our lips never parted until we reached my suite. Taking my key card from my pocket, I waved it over the lock and opened the door. She stepped inside first, her back turned to me as I softly stroked my tongue across her shoulder while my fingers unzipped her dress. A soft moan escaped her lips as I pulled her dress from her body. Her supple and perky breasts were bare, and her perfectly round ass was dressed in nothing but a white thong, making my cock even harder than it already was. My mouth explored her neck as my hands fondled her breasts. With the slight turn of her head, our lips met. Picking her up, I carried her to the bedroom and laid her down on the bed. Hovering over her, I traced the outline of her breast with my finger.

"While I undress, I want you to play with yourself. Can you do that for me?"

"Yes," she answered with a whisper.

Taking her hand, I slipped two of her fingers in my mouth.

"Are you ready?"

"Yes." A small smile crossed her lips.

I climbed off and slowly removed her panties. As I stood at the end of the bed, I removed my wallet from my pants, took out a condom, and tossed it on the bed. Her fingers roamed down her torso and to her sweet spot. I watched as she pleasured herself while I stripped out of my clothes. The light moans that escaped her was too much to bear. I needed to finish the job for her, taste her and then bury my cock deep inside her.

"Let me." I smiled as my fingers took their place and my tongue slowly slid up her inner thigh.

❧

*A*spen

My body was on fire while my skin trembled at his touch. The way his tongue and fingers explored my sensitive area was pure mastery. I'd never been so turned on or tuned into my body like I was at that moment. Exhilaration soared through me as my sexual moans grew deeper. As amazing as he made me feel, I knew the best was yet to come for he was more than blessed in the goods department. He touched me in ways I had never been touched before, pushing my body into an earth-shattering orgasm. Throwing my head back, I let out a howl as the intensity tore through me like never before. He lifted his head and smiled at me as he grabbed the condom from the bed, tore open the package with his teeth and then rolled it over his hard cock. Hovering over me, he pushed himself inside inch by inch as deep moans escaped his lips. He thrust in and out of me with slow smooth strokes. His mouth met mine, and as our lips twisted with pleasure and with every thrust, my body headed for O-Town once again. My fingers dug into the flesh of his skin as our moans synced together and we both arrived at the big O at the same time.

"Fuck," he moaned before collapsing on top of me.

I smiled as he buried his face into the side of my neck and my body slowly came down from the adrenaline rush. He lifted his head and pushed a strand of hair from my face.

"That was incredible." He grinned.

"It was very incredible." I grinned back.

His eyes stared into mine for a moment before he climbed off me and went into the bathroom.

"Stay with me tonight," he said as he walked back into the bedroom. "Unless you have to get back to your sister-and brother-in-law."

"No. I don't have to get back to them. But I need to send my sister a text message or else she'll worry and do something stupid like call the police."

He chuckled. "Where's your phone? I'll go get it for you."

"My purse is wherever I dropped it in the living area."

A moment later, he walked in and handed me my purse. Pulling out my phone, I saw I had a missed call from her and two text messages.

"Lucas and I went to the bar, and you weren't there. I called, and you didn't answer. You're not in your room. What is going on?"

"Now I'm worried and if I don't hear from you, I'll assume someone has kidnapped you and I'm calling the police."

"I'm fine. Sorry. I'm with someone. I'll explain everything in the morning. Good night."

Within seconds, a message from her came through.

"Who the hell are you with? Are you okay? Tell me where you're at and Lucas and I will come get you."

"Trust me, G, I've never been better. I'm here in the hotel. Stop worrying. I'll see you in the morning."

"She's freaking out, isn't she?" Elijah asked.

"Yeah. Something like that." I smiled as I set my phone on the nightstand and rolled over.

Before I knew it, his arm was tucked tightly around me. I lay there, waiting for him to fall sound asleep before making my escape. As amazing and mind blowing as the sex was, it was time for us to part ways before the alcohol wore off and I realized what I'd done with a complete stranger in Hawaii.

CHAPTER 5

*A*spen

My eyes shot open and when I looked at the clock on the nightstand, it was three a.m. Shit. I must have fallen asleep while I waited for him to go to sleep. His arm was no longer around me, and he was facing the other way. Thank God. It would be a lot easier to escape that way. Carefully climbing out of bed, I grabbed my phone, purse and panties and tiptoed out to the living area. Slipping on my dress, I grabbed my shoes and cautiously opened the door, stepped out into the hallway and then quietly closed the door behind me. I ran down the hall to the elevator, pushed the button, and the doors immediately opened. I let out a sigh of relief as I stepped inside.

I pulled my key card from my purse and quietly opened the door to my room. As I tiptoed inside, my sister's voice scared the shit out of me.

"You have some explaining to do, little sister," Geneva said as she flipped the light switch on the wall and stood there with her arms folded.

"Why are you up?" I whispered as not to wake up Lucas.

"I couldn't sleep because I was worried about you. Where the hell have you been?"

"With a guy." I grinned as I set down my shoes and my purse.

"I kind of figured that. What guy and why?"

"His name is Elijah. I bumped into him as I was walking out of the bathroom. He found me sitting at the bar, bought my drinks, and then we went up to his suite."

"You had sex with a guy you met at the bar? Who are you?" She smirked.

"I did, and it was amazing." I grinned. "Oh my God, G, you should see him. He's not only gorgeous, he's sexy as hell. I have never laid eyes on a man so sexy in my life. The minute I saw him, I got all the feels if you know what I mean." I smiled as I raised my brow.

"And the sex?" she asked.

"Mind blowing. To be honest, I didn't even think it was possible for my body to react the way it did when he touched me."

"What is going on?" Lucas yawned as he walked into the room.

"Aspen had sex with a hot guy she met at the bar and she's giving me the juicy details."

"Ugh. I'm going back to bed. Glad you're safe, Aspen. You both realize we have a flight to catch in four hours, right?"

"Yeah. Yeah. Go back to bed, grumpy," Geneva spoke as she waved her hand. "I want to hear more." She smiled as she grabbed me and led me to the couch."

❧

*E*lijah

I opened my eyes and saw the empty space next to me. She must have left in the middle of the night. Why? I was hoping for one last round with her before I headed back to New York.

"Bro, are you up?" I heard Nathan's voice as he knocked on the door.

Climbing out of bed, I slipped on my pajama bottoms and opened the door.

"I am now and I'm sure everyone else on this floor is. Come on in."

As I went to shut the door, Mason stopped it with his hand.

"Let's go get some breakfast. I'm starving."

"Yeah. Maybe your new friend from the bar can join us." Nathan smirked.

"She's gone."

"She left already?" Mason looked at his watch.

"She snuck out in the middle of the night."

"Damn, Elijah. You're losing your game," Mason spoke. "Women don't leave you in the middle of the night. It's usually the other way around."

"I know."

"She is one hell of a looker though." Nathan grinned.

"Yeah. She is." A light smile crossed my face. "I'm taking a quick shower and then we can go down for breakfast."

I stood in the shower and let the warm water run down me as I thought about her. The sexual chemistry between us was incredible and unlike anything I'd ever experienced before. No woman had ever snuck out on me in the middle of the night, and I found myself pissed off because she did. After I finished my shower, I threw on some clothes and stormed out into the room, opened the door, and looked back at my brothers who were just standing there.

"What the fuck are you waiting for? I thought you were starving," I snapped.

"Bro, what's your problem?" Mason asked.

"He's finally realizing how pissed he is that the girl left in the middle of night." Nathan laughed.

"Fuck you both. Let's go."

*A*spen
　　I flew in from Hawaii last night, and today was my first day back to work since the death of my father. I welcomed the distraction even though I still had a lot to do.

"You wanted to see me, Charlie?" I asked as I stepped into my boss's office.

"Welcome back. How are you doing?"

"I'm okay." I took a seat in the chair across from his desk. "You know, I expected to see a lot of case files on my desk when I got in."

"That's what I want to talk to you about. We're transferring you to Bankruptcy Law starting today.

"What? Why?"

"Listen, Aspen, I'll be honest with you and I'm not holding anything back because I completely respect you. You working directly for me is causing a problem in my marriage."

"What?" I let out a light laugh for I thought he was joking.

"My wife doesn't feel comfortable with us working together. She said you're too beautiful, and she has issues with it."

I sat there in shock and disbelief that this conversation was happening.

"Your wife's insecurities in your marriage shouldn't have an effect on my job. Charlie, this is ridiculous."

"I agree, Aspen, but there's nothing I can do. If I want my marriage to stay intact, I have to do what's best for it."

"I'm one of your best lawyers in this firm. I'm a trial lawyer, not a paper pusher behind a desk all day. I didn't go to Yale and graduate at the top of my class to do bankruptcy law."

"I know that and I'm sorry. I really am. But I need you to understand my position here."

"Your position is that you're a man who cheated on his wife a few years back and she doesn't trust you anymore and she never will. And because of your infidelities, my life gets turned upside down? No thanks, Charlie." I stood up. "I don't want to work at a firm where the owner's wife dictates who can and can't work here based on their looks. I quit, and I will sue you and this firm."

"Come on, Aspen. Don't jump into anything you'll regret."

"Regret?" I laughed. "You'll be the one regretting your decision. You know better than this, Charlie. Do yourself a favor and just get divorced already. Oh wait, you won't because it'll cost you too much money between half the firm, your bank accounts, vacation homes, alimony and child support. Typical man." I shook my head as I stormed out of his office, grabbed my things, and got the hell out of there.

I was furious. So furious I couldn't see straight. The moment I got into the car, I pulled my phone from my purse and dialed my friend, Joe.

CHAPTER 6

*a*spen

"I can't believe it, Aspen," Geneva said as we spoke over FaceTime.

"Now I'm out of a job."

"Listen, don't take this the wrong way, but I'm kind of glad it happened."

"What? How can you say that?"

"Think about it for a minute. What has always been your dream besides going to law school?"

"Working for a top-notch law firm in New York City." I smiled.

"Exactly. Only you couldn't do that because you stayed home to take care of Dad. Now that he's gone and you have no job, what's keeping you there in Connecticut? Nothing, that's what. You have me and Lucas in New York and we want you here. You can move in with us until you find an apartment and get a job. I need you here and you need me too. Admit it. There's no reason to stay in Connecticut anymore. You even said when we were in Hawaii that you were thinking about putting the house up for sale. Do it and move to New York. Start fresh. You love it here."

"I'll think about it. I have so much going on right now. Let me clear my head."

"Well, hurry it up." She smiled. "I have to go. I need to hop on a conference call. I love you."

"I love you too, sis."

I went into the kitchen to clean up the dishes from breakfast, and as I was rinsing them and loading the dishwasher, I thought about Elijah. A smile crossed my lips as my body tingled with thoughts of our magical night together. It was a nice memory, and I was glad that I had it. I would admit that I regretted sneaking out. One more round with him would have been the icing on the cake.

A knock on the door startled me out of my fantasy. Drying my hands, I opened the door and saw Ron standing there. Instantly, I shut it and began to walk away when I heard it open again and he stepped inside.

"What part of the door slamming in your face do you not understand?" I spoke as I turned around.

"Aspen, I just want to talk. I don't like the way we left things."

"Too bad for you, Ron. I love the way we left things and the way my shoe hit you when you walked out the door. Now please leave."

"No. Not until you hear what I have to say."

"You cheated and broke up with me at my father's funeral. You didn't even have the decency to wait another day. I don't want to hear anything you have to say."

"I know. I'm an asshole. A huge asshole and I'm sorry."

"Fine. You're sorry." I rolled my eyes as I walked into the kitchen and wiped down the counters.

"You want to know the real reason I broke up with you?"

"Enlighten me, please," I said.

"Because you pushed me away. You never made time for us. You were always busy with your cases and taking care of your dad. Shit. I was lucky if we had sex every other week. I was hoping things would change, but they didn't. I have needs too."

"And you got those needs fulfilled by someone else."

"Listen, you're an amazing woman, but you never let me in. Not completely. You told me that day that you gave me your heart. No, you didn't, Aspen. Sometimes I felt like I was a stranger to you."

I sighed as I set down the rag, walked into the living room and took a seat on the couch.

"Why are you telling me all this, Ron?"

"Because I love you. I always will and I just want you to be happy. I think you loved me too, but it was only ever as a friend." He sat down next to me.

I was ashamed to admit he was right.

"I'm sorry." I laid my head on his shoulder. "I didn't mean to make you feel like that."

"It's okay. I realized that it just wasn't in the cards for us, and I know you knew it too. Probably sooner than I did. But that doesn't mean we can't be friends."

"I'd like that." I smiled as I lifted my head from his shoulder. "I have some news."

"What?"

"I'm going to fulfill my dream and go to work for a top-notch law firm in New York."

"You're moving?"

"Yeah. I think I am. There's no reason for me to stay in Connecticut anymore and I want to be close to Geneva and Lucas. It's time to put my plan in motion."

"I'll miss you, but I'm happy for you. You'll do really well in New York." Ron smiled as he kissed the side of my head. "I better go."

We both stood up and headed towards the door.

"Ron?"

"Yeah?"

"Thanks for coming over and telling me the truth."

"You're welcome. Good luck and promise me you'll stay in touch."

"I will." I smiled as he walked out the door.

"Looks like I'm moving to New York," I said out loud as I turned on some music and began dancing.

One Week Later

I stood outside the law firm with two legal envelopes in my hand. Taking in a deep breath, I walked inside and straight to Charlie's office.

"I knew you'd come back after you calmed down." He smiled. "Have a seat and let's talk."

"Yes, let's talk." I smirked as I placed the first envelope on his desk and slid it to him.

"What's this?" He picked it up and opened it. "You're serious about suing me?"

"I haven't filed yet because I know we can work out a monetary agreement like we lawyers do."

"You're not getting a dime, Aspen. I'll hire you back for the bankruptcy department. Take it or leave it. But that's all you're getting."

"Is that so? Aren't you the least bit curious what is in this envelope?" I held it up.

He nervously shifted in his seat.

"Let me show you." I smiled as I took out the photos of him and a woman who was not his wife entering a hotel with their arms around each other.

"What the fuck! Where did you get those?"

"I have my sources. You should know that. I wonder what your wife would say if these appeared in your mailbox. Or better yet, if I hand delivered them during the day while you're here at the office."

"You wouldn't dare."

"Actually, I would. You were willing to disrupt my life and take away a job I love because your wife can't trust you around beautiful women. And with good reason by the looks of these photos. Since you were so honest with me about her demands, let me be honest with you. This woman you're with, I'm not sure what you see in her, but your wife is way prettier."

"What do you want, Aspen?" he scowled.

"A full year's salary plus my bonus. After I get it, you can tear up the lawsuit. As for the photos, they're yours, and you won't see me again."

"How do I know you don't have copies?"

"You have my word. I just want this over with so I can move on. What you did was wrong."

He glared at me as he leaned back in his chair. I could see the wheels spinning in his head. He had no choice, and he knew it.

"Fine. I'll be right back." He sighed as he got up from his chair and walked out of his office.

About fifteen minutes later, he returned and handed me a white envelope. I opened it and took out the check made payable to me in one lump sum.

"Thank you." I handed him the photos. "It's been a pleasure working for you, Charlie." I smirked.

"Just leave, Aspen." He shook his head.

CHAPTER 7

*E*lijah

"How's the Cox case coming along?" My mother asked as she stepped into my office.

"Good. We go to trial next week."

"Excellent. What did you think about our last interview candidate? What was her name again?" She cocked her head.

"Angelica." I smiled. "I thought she was great."

"Because you were thinking with the wrong head." Her brow raised.

I sighed as I leaned back in my chair.

"I felt none of them were a right fit for the firm," she spoke.

"What was wrong with Angelica?"

"Beside the fact that she graduated at the bottom of her class, all kinds of things. You would have noticed that if you would have checked her resume instead of checking out her tits."

"For God's sake, Mother. Like you're one to talk. I'm surprised you didn't offer that Jaden guy the job. I saw the way you were ogling him like a lovesick puppy dog."

"I know." She smirked. "As handsome as he was, his resume wasn't up to par for this firm. Anyway, we have someone coming in tomorrow at ten a.m. for an interview. She's from Connecticut. Make sure you're available."

"I'll be there."

"Don't forget family dinner is tonight at seven."

"I haven't forgotten."

❧

J climbed out of the cab that pulled up to the curb of my mother's townhouse on East 92nd street. Opening the front door, I stepped inside, and the smell of my mother's homemade lasagna infiltrated the air. Walking into the kitchen, I found her bending over the oven while Nathan tossed the salad and Mason set the table.

"Sorry I'm a few minutes late. I got held up at the office and traffic was terrible."

"That's okay, darling." My mother smiled. "You boys grab yourself a drink and sit down at the table."

I walked over to the bar and poured three scotches. One for me and each of my brothers. Thursday nights was always family dinner night, and we had to make sure we were available. Except for Nathan with his flight schedules. But when he was home, he never missed a meal. A majority of the time my mother cooked, and when she didn't feel like it, we went out to a restaurant. The rule was that family dinner was just for the four of us, regardless if we were seeing anyone. It had always been just us. My father took off when Mason was born, leaving my mother a single parent. I was four when he left, and I really didn't remember him too much.

"So, Nathan, you start," my mother spoke. "What's going on in your life?"

"Nothing much, Mom. Just jetting from place to place, like always."

"Are you seeing anyone?" she asked.

"A few women here and there." He smirked.

"And how about you, Mason?"

"Same. A few women here and there."

29

"How's life at the fire station?"

"It's good, Mom. Putting out a lot of fires."

"Well, you know how I feel about your line of work. It's dangerous."

"It's a pure adrenaline rush." He smiled. "And you don't think Nathan's job is dangerous being a pilot?"

"Yes, I do. I worry about you boys every day."

"Come on, Mom. You don't worry about Elijah. Do you?" Nathan asked.

"He's a lawyer, Nathan. I need not worry about him. Now, I want to hear all about your trip to Hawaii."

"Careful, Mom." Nathan smiled. "That's a touchy subject with Elijah."

"Shut up!" I threw a roll at him.

"Why? What happened?" she asked.

"Elijah met some smoking hot chick at the hotel bar and took her up to his suite. She snuck out in the middle of the night. No goodbye. No note. Nothing." Mason laughed.

"He was so pissed off the next day that he took it out on us," Nathan said.

"I did not. Don't listen to them."

"Why would she sneak out like that, darling?"

"How the hell do I know? I asked her to stay the night, and she agreed. I woke up the next morning and she was gone."

"Well, it doesn't matter. You knew you'd never see her again."

"No, but it sure as hell bruised his ego," Nathan spoke with laughter.

I sighed as I sipped my drink.

"It happens. I've done it before. Now leave Elijah alone."

After we finished eating, the three of us helped clean up and then it was time to go.

"Thanks for dinner, Mom." Nathan kissed her cheek.

"You're welcome, darling. Have a safe flight tomorrow."

"Thanks, Mom. I love you," Mason said as he kissed her cheek.

"I love you too, Mason."

"Bye, Mom. Thanks for dinner. I'll see you in the morning." I kissed her cheek.

As soon as I stepped off the elevator and into the foyer of my penthouse, I took off my suit coat and poured myself a drink. All that talk about Hawaii had me thinking about her again. Damn it. I didn't need to think about her. I had work to do and a case to prepare for.

CHAPTER 8

*A*spen

I arrived in New York and took a cab to my sister's Upper East Side apartment. She had no idea that I was coming let alone moving here. When she asked me the other day if I'd made my decision, I told her I was still thinking about it for I wanted to surprise her and Lucas.

Donnie, the doorman smiled as he held the door open while I rolled in my two large suitcases with my carryon bag strapped to the handle.

"It's wonderful to see you again, Aspen."

"Thanks, Donnie. It's good to see you too."

"Your sister didn't tell me you were coming for a visit."

"She doesn't know. It's a surprise. And I'm not visiting this time. I have officially moved here."

"Excellent news!" He grinned as he pushed the button to the elevator.

The doors opened, and I stepped inside, taking it up to the eleventh floor. I stood in front of her apartment door, lightly knocked and anxiously waited for her to open it.

"OH MY GOD!" she screamed as she jumped up and down before hugging me tight. "Lucas, Aspen is here! Tell me you're here to stay."

"I'm here to stay." I grinned.

"Welcome to New York, Aspen." Lucas kissed my cheek and took my luggage from me.

"I can't believe you're here and you didn't tell me you were for sure moving," Geneva spoke as she handed me a glass of wine.

"I wanted it to be a surprise. Guess what?"

"What?"

"I have a job interview tomorrow."

"Oh my God, already? Where?"

"Wolfe & Associates over on East 82nd Street." I grinned.

"Are you serious? They're one of the biggest law firms in New York."

"I know. It shocked me when they called."

"And if you don't get the job?" she pouted.

"There are thousands of law firms here. I'll keep applying."

❧

I entered through the doors of the building on East 82nd Street and took the elevator up to the 37th floor. When the doors opened, I stepped onto the black & white mosaic marble floor and a young blonde woman sitting behind a mahogany desk greeted me.

"Can I help you?" She cheerfully smiled.

"I'm here for an interview with Caitlin Wolfe."

"Are you, Aspen Michaelson?"

"Yes."

"Have a seat please and I'll let her assistant know you're here."

I took a seat on the elongated couch, crossed my legs, and nervously tapped my foot. The firm I worked for in Connecticut was big, but this—this was bigger and better.

"Hi, Miss Michaelson, I'm Amy, Ms. Wolfe's assistant. Follow me and I'll take you to her office. May I get you some coffee or water?"

"No thank you. I'm good."

She led me down the hallway until we stopped in front of a large mahogany door. Placing her hand on the handle, she slowly opened it and announced my arrival.

"Miss Michaelson is here for her interview," she spoke.

"Excellent. Send her in."

The moment I stepped inside, the woman behind the desk stood up and the man sitting in the chair across from her desk turned his head and looked at me. I swallowed hard as our eyes locked and a sick feeling in the pit of my belly emerged.

Oh God. My one-night stand from Hawaii was sitting there and probably thinks I'm a whore.

"Miss Michaelson, it's nice to meet you. I'm Caitlin Wolfe." She extended her hand as she walked over to me.

"It's nice to meet you." I placed my hand in hers.

"This is my son, Elijah. He'll be sitting in on the interview with us."

He walked over with a small smile across his lips and extended his hand to me.

"It's nice to meet you, Miss Michaelson." He cocked his head.

"The pleasure is all mine, Mr. Wolfe."

He was pretending we'd never met, and I needed to play along.

"Please, have a seat." He gestured.

The nervousness I'd already felt magnified as I took the seat next to him.

"I must say I am highly impressed with your resume," Caitlin spoke. "I see you're from Connecticut. Am I to assume you're moving to New York?"

"I already have. I got in yesterday and I'm staying with my sister until I find an apartment."

She slowly nodded her head as she held my resume in her hands.

"You're a Yale graduate with honors and you previously worked for Charlie Connors."

"Yes." I glanced over at Elijah who was staring at me.

"Why did you leave his firm?"

"I've always wanted to work for a large firm in New York. That was my plan when I graduated law school, but then my father became ill and I stayed in Connecticut to take care of him. My sister and her husband were already here, so I really had no choice."

"That's very admirable of you. I'd hope my boys would do the same for me." She smirked at Elijah. "There's one thing that is bothering me. I have a friend who works in the tax department over at Connors, Platt & Associates, so I called her. Her name is Mariana. Perhaps you know her?"

"Yes. I know Mariana." I nervously smiled.

"She told me you abruptly quit without notice. She said she saw you storming out of Mr. Connor's office the day you quit. Care to explain why?"

Damn her.

"Mr. Connors and I had a disagreement."

"So you just up and quit over a disagreement?" Her brow raised.

"What was the disagreement about?" Elijah asked.

"I'd rather not say." I bit down on my bottom lip as I looked down at my hands.

"Miss Michaelson, you're up against some other candidates for the one position we have open. I need your total honesty if you want me to consider you," Caitlin spoke. "Abruptly quitting your previous job without giving notice doesn't look good. It speaks very little about your professionalism. How am I to know that you wouldn't do the same here if we hired you and had a disagreement?"

Okay then. She already thought I was unprofessional, so I'd have nothing to lose by telling her the truth. Apparently, Mariana already blew it for me. I placed my hands on the arms of the chair and rose from my seat.

"Fine. You want to know why I quit? Because I'm too pretty."

"Excuse me?" Both her and Elijah spoke at the same time.

I paced around her office. It was unprofessional, but I wasn't getting the job anyway. Especially since I'd slept with Elijah in Hawaii. I was sure he'd see to that.

"Charlie's wife told him I was too beautiful, and she didn't feel comfortable with us working together. So he decided to transfer me

35

to bankruptcy law. I'm a damn good lawyer and I didn't deserve that because of his wife's insecurities. It's not my fault he's a cheater, and she doesn't trust him."

"Interesting." Caitlin smiled. "Sit down and tell me more. What did you say to him?"

"I told him no and that his marriage issues had nothing to do with me. He didn't care and said that he needed to do as his wife said for the sake of his marriage, so I quit."

"And you just left it at that?" Elijah asked.

"No. I drew up the paperwork for a lawsuit."

"Did you file it?" Caitlin asked.

"No. I went another route first."

"And that was?" Elijah asked.

"I had him followed one night because I knew he was cheating on his wife again. Some pictures turned up of him and another woman entering a hotel. I brought him the lawsuit and told him I wouldn't file if we worked out a monetary agreement. He laughed and said no way, so I handed over the photos."

"This is good." Caitlin grinned. "Then what?"

"He panicked. So I told him I wanted a year's worth of pay plus my bonus and then I'd quietly leave, and the pictures would stay with him."

"So you blackmailed him?" Elijah asked.

"I did. I'm not ashamed and I will not apologize for it. What he did was wrong."

"You're a little spitfire." Caitlin smirked. "What you did was unethical, but to be honest, I'd probably have done the same thing if I was in your shoes. That was risky and being a good lawyer involves taking risks. Miss Michaelson, I believe you're exactly what this firm needs. There are times this firm plays dirty. Just ask Elijah." She smiled. "He's the master at it."

I glanced over and gave him a small smile.

"So, if you're interested in working for us, the job is yours and you can start tomorrow." She smiled.

"Thank you, Mrs. Wolfe."

"It's Ms. and just call me Caitlin. Elijah will show you around. Plan on being here tomorrow morning at eight a.m. Now, if you'll both excuse me, I have a lunch date with a client. Welcome to Wolfe and Associates, Miss Michaelson. I know you'll fit in just fine." She extended her hand.

"Thank you again, Caitlin. I look forward to working with you." I smiled.

She walked out of the office and left me standing there alone with Elijah.

"Well, isn't this quite a surprise," I said as I looked at him.

"It certainly is. I had no idea you were a lawyer."

"And I had no idea you were one either. It's not like we really did any talking that night."

"No. We didn't."

CHAPTER 9

*E*lijah

I couldn't believe she was standing in front of me, and I couldn't believe my mother hired her. Shit. She looked just as beautiful standing before me as she did the night I first saw her in Hawaii. But regardless of how she looked, it still pissed me off that she snuck out in the middle of the night.

"Is this going to be weird?" she asked. "I don't want things to be weird between us."

"What? The fact that we fucked one night in Hawaii with the notion we'd never see each other again? Yeah, it is kind of weird, but we'll just have to get over it. I want to make something very clear. What happened between us in Hawaii was a one-time thing and it won't happen again. Understand me?"

"That's so odd." She cocked her head at me.

"What is?"

"I was just going to tell you the same thing. I have rules about dating in the workplace."

"Nobody said anything about dating."

"I know. The same rule applies to sex."

"Good. Now that we got that out of the way, I'll show you around and introduce you to your secretary."

I walked out of the office and she followed behind as I introduced her to the staff and took her to her office.

"Colleen, I'd like you to meet your new boss, Aspen Michaelson. Aspen, this is Colleen, your secretary."

"It's nice to meet you, Miss Michaelson." She grinned.

"It's nice to meet you, Colleen. Please, just call me Aspen."

"Aspen will start tomorrow morning, so make sure everything is set up for her."

"I will, Elijah."

We stood inside her office and she looked around.

"The courthouse is within walking distance from here. When my mother started this firm, she did it with the intention that we'd have quick and easy access to the court building."

"Smart woman." She smiled.

"She's very smart. Now if you'll excuse me, I need to get back to work." I pulled my phone out of my pocket. "I need your phone number. We all work closely and since you'll be working directly under me, I must be able to get ahold of you at all times."

"Yes. Of course."

As she rattled it off, I saved it and then sent her a text message. "I just sent you a text, so you'll have my number. I'll see you tomorrow morning."

I headed back to my office and Marie followed me inside.

"She's a beautiful woman, Elijah." She smiled.

"And? What's your point, Marie?" I asked with irritation.

"Just saying you need to mind your manners."

"Too late. That's the woman I slept with in Hawaii."

"The one who snuck out in the middle of the night?"

"Yep."

"Oh. This will be good." She grinned as she walked out of my office.

I sighed as I opened the file sitting on my desk.

I looked up and saw my mother walking past my office.

"Mother, can you come in here for a moment?" I shouted.

"What is it, Elijah?" she asked with a smile.

"Shut the door, please." I set my pen down and leaned back in my chair. "I want to discuss the hiring of Aspen Michaelson."

"What about it?" she asked as she sat down across my desk.

"You were very quick to hire her without even discussing it with me first. You've never done that before. Usually you dismiss the potential candidate and then we discuss it. We always make a joint decision."

"Do you have a problem with Aspen?" She raised her brow.

I looked down, picked up my pen and fiddled with it, hesitating with my response.

"No. That's not the point."

"I honestly don't see what the problem is, Elijah. Aspen is a beautiful and smart woman. Don't tell me there's no way you would have objected to hiring her."

"I would have said no."

"Why?" She laughed. "You don't even know her. Wait a minute—do you know her?" Her steadily narrowed eye glared at me. "I saw your reaction when she walked through the door. I also noticed the way she kept looking at you. And it wasn't in the 'I think you're hot and sexy way,' it was as if she knew you. Don't lie to your mother, Elijah. I've taught you better than that."

"Fine!" I threw my pen across the desk. "She's the woman I met in Hawaii."

"The woman who snuck out on you in the middle of the night?"

"Yes."

She began to laugh as she got up from her chair and headed towards the door.

"I knew I liked her. Get over it, Elijah, and keep your ego out of the office. Save it for the courtroom." She opened the door and walked out.

CHAPTER 10

a spen

I walked out of the building, placed my hand on my belly, and let out the biggest breath of my life. This wasn't possible, but yet it happened. If I thought he was sexy as sin in Hawaii, he was even sexier now in that damn tailored designer suit he wore. Shit. The moment I saw him, my body instantly trembled, remembering what he'd done to me that night. Shit. Shit. Shit.

As the cab pulled up to Geneva's apartment building, and I climbed out, Donnie held the door open for me.

"How's your day going, Aspen?"

"I got a job." I grinned.

"Congratulations. Where at?"

"Wolfe & Associates Law Firm."

"Wow. They're one of the biggest firms in New York."

"I know. Now that I got that secured, I need to look for an apartment."

"I think today just may be your lucky day." He smiled. "Unit 402 just opened up. If I were you, I'd go straight into the office and talk to Charlene."

"Oh, my God. I would love to live here. I'll go see her right now. Thanks, Donnie." I smiled as I kissed his cheek.

I talked to Charlene, and she took me up to apartment 402 for a tour.

"This is a two bedroom, 1 ½ bath unit," she spoke as we stepped inside.

The entire apartment was white. White walls, white kitchen and white oak flooring throughout. It was perfect, right down to the white quartz countertops in the kitchen and marble flooring in the bathroom. But the one thing that immediately sold me about the apartment were the oversized custom seven-foot windows throughout the place.

"I'll take it." I grinned.

"Excellent. Let's go back to the office and I'll get the paperwork started. Once you're approved, you can move in." She smiled.

My second day in New York and already my life was on the upswing. Except for the fact that I would be working for Elijah Wolfe. A man who made my insides burn with desire every time I saw him.

I went up to Geneva's apartment, poured myself a glass of wine and sat down on the couch. All I could think about was him and how awkward it was going to be working at the law firm where I'd see and have interaction with him every single day. He was different. He seemed kind of cold and almost as if he couldn't get away from me fast enough. My rule about dating in the workplace was false. I'd only said that because of what he said about sex never happening again. He didn't like that his mother hired me. That much I could tell. Oh well. He'd have to get over it because I wasn't going anywhere. I would not let him crush my dream.

The ringing of my phone startled me, and when I answered it, Charlene's voice was on the other end.

"Hello."

"Aspen, it's Charlene. Congratulations, you have been approved for the apartment. All I need you to do is come down at your convenience to sign the lease and pay the first month's rent and security deposit and I'll hand over your keys."

"That's great, Charlene. Can I come down now?"

"Of course. I'll be waiting."

I did a little happy dance as I finished off my wine, grabbed my purse and my checkbook and headed down to Charlene's office.

I browsed the furniture store and picked out all new furniture for my apartment. While I was in the bedroom section, my phone rang, and Geneva was calling.

"Hello."

"Where are you? I haven't heard from you all day."

"I'm running a couple of errands."

"What happened at the interview? I expected a call or a text."

"I'll be home soon, and I'll tell you all about it."

"Well, hurry up. Lucas is cooking his famous pasta and meatballs."

"I will. I'm just wrapping up. Talk to you soon."

After completing my furniture purchase and getting the delivery scheduled, I headed back to the apartment.

"Honey, I'm home," I announced as I stepped through the door.

"Oh, my God. Where have you been? I don't see any bags in your hands. What the hell have you been doing all day?" Geneva asked.

I kicked off my shoes, reached in my purse and took out the keys to my new place.

"I got an apartment today." I grinned.

"Already?" She gave me a pouty look. "Where? I hope it's somewhere close by."

"It is." I continued to grin. In fact, it's right here in the building. Unit 402."

She grabbed me as she screamed and we both jumped up and down.

"How? I didn't know a unit was available. I've been checking."

"Apparently, it just opened up today. Donnie told me when I came back from my interview."

"Congratulations, Aspen." Lucas smiled as he kissed my cheek and handed me a glass of wine.

"Thanks, Lucas."

"What about the interview? How did it go?"

"I start tomorrow!"

"AH!" she screamed again.

"As exciting as it is, there's one problem with it," I spoke as I took a seat at the table.

"What?"

"Elijah works there, and I'll be working for him."

She sat across from me with a perplexed look on her face.

"Who's Elijah?"

"I believe he's the guy from Hawaii," Lucas chimed in.

"What?!" Geneva exclaimed. "Oh, Aspen. Damn. That must have been a shock."

"To say the least." I stabbed a meatball with my fork. "Trust me. He was just as shocked as I was. His mother, Caitlin Wolfe, is the owner of the firm."

"So what did he say to you?"

"He told me what happened in Hawaii was a one-time thing and it would never happen again." I smiled as I shoved a meatball in my mouth. "He just wanted to make that very clear."

"What a dick. How did you respond?"

"I told him I agreed because I have a rule about office dating."

"You don't have any such rule."

"I know. But I wasn't going to let him think he was in control."

CHAPTER 11

*E*lijah

    I left the office and went next door to Rudy's bar where I met Mason for a drink.

"Hey, Elijah." Hanna, the bartender flirted. "The usual?"

"Hanna." I nodded. "Yeah. I'll be over at that table with my brother."

She gave me a smile and a wink, and I walked over to where Mason sat.

"Hey, bro," he said as he took a sip of his drink.

"You will never believe what happened today."

Hanna walked over and set my scotch in front of me.

"Thanks, darling." I winked at her.

Mason and I both watched as she walked away in her short tight black skirt that barely covered her ass.

"What happened?" Mason asked.

"Mom hired a new lawyer for the firm today." I picked up my glass.

"And?" His brow arched.

"She hired Aspen Michaelson."

"Should I know that name?"

"Aspen? Ring any bells?"

"Shit. Not the woman you slept with in Hawaii?"

"Yes. Her." I threw back my drink.

"Damn." He laughed. "I didn't know she was a lawyer."

"Me either. Mom loved her. She hired her right on the spot."

"You're fucked." He grinned as he pointed his finger at me. "Did you tell her you didn't appreciate her sneaking out in the middle of the night?"

"No. But I told her what happened between us was a one-time thing and it would never happen again."

"What did she say to that?"

"She agreed and told me she has rules about office dating."

I finished my drink, and Hanna gave me a nod as I held up my empty glass.

"She's beautiful and smart. How are you going to handle that?" he asked.

"I'll handle it like I always do. The only thing between us in Hawaii were the bed sheets. She was a great fuck, and that was it. Nothing more than a stranger I met at the hotel bar."

"She's not a stranger anymore, Elijah. She's your employee now. See, this is always why when you travel you find out where the girl is from. Maybe if you knew she was from New York, you wouldn't have slept with her."

"She isn't from New York. She's from Connecticut and just moved here yesterday."

"Damn. What are the odds?" He shook his head as he finished his drink.

I got up from my chair and patted him on the back.

"I have to go. I have to prepare for a closing tomorrow."

I left the bar and headed home. Taking a seat in my study, I opened my laptop and searched Aspen Michaelson. Her picture came up as an associate at her previous law firm. I stared at it and couldn't get the images of our night together out of my head. I started to get hard, so hard I needed to release the throbbing sensation that filled inside me.

Once I finished, I closed my laptop, grabbed my notepad, and took it out to the living room. After I poured myself a scotch, I began working on my closing argument for court tomorrow. I wasn't sure how I would deal with Aspen tomorrow.

CHAPTER 12

*a*spen

There was something to be said about the simple act of dancing. Not only did it release feel-good endorphins making a person feel alive, it stimulated confidence. My mother told me I danced in her womb and I never stopped, even after I was born. I'd been dancing my entire life. I wasn't talking about professional dancing or taking dance classes. I was talking about free dancing. Whenever and wherever I needed to. I discovered at the mere age of eight that dancing played a significant role in my life. It calmed me down and cleared my head when I was stressed out, nervous, or depressed about something.

I'd gotten the lead role in a school play. It was the first time I had to stand up and perform in front of an entire crowd. I didn't think I could do it. My mind rambled on and on with scenarios of me screwing up and the audience laughing at me. It petrified me. Then, on the night of the play, I turned on some music, stood in front of the mirror, and began moving my body. I danced around my room to the beat and just let go of everything that I feared. I nailed the play and received a standing ovation. That was a big deal for anyone. But to an eight-year-old, it was magical. That was the night I discovered the true power of dancing for any situation in my life.

I nervously stood in front of the mirror in my black tailored skirt suit. The only reason I was nervous was because of Elijah. I didn't like his reaction to seeing me and I had a feeling he wouldn't feel any different today. I turned on some music and began moving my shoulders to the beat while staring at myself in the mirror. Suddenly, the door to my room opened and Geneva came dancing in and grabbed my hand. We danced around the room for a few minutes and then it was time for me to leave.

"You'll do great." She smiled.

"I know." I grinned.

I put on my heels, grabbed my briefcase, and headed out the door. The one perfect thing about working at Wolfe & Associates was the fact that it was only a ten-minute walk from my apartment.

⚜

*A*fter stopping at Starbucks and grabbing a coffee, I entered the building and took the elevator up to the offices.

"Good morning, Colleen." I smiled before walking into my office.

"Good morning, Aspen." She followed me inside. "Welcome to Wolfe & Associates."

"Thank you."

I set my briefcase down and took a seat behind my new desk, looking around at the space before me.

"I'm a bit of a busybody and I know everything that goes on in this firm. So, if there's anything you want to know, just ask." She grinned. "And just so you know, you can trust me. Your secrets are my secrets."

"I will definitely keep that in mind." I smiled as she walked out.

"You made it," Elijah spoke as he stood outside my office door.

"Why wouldn't I?" My brow raised.

"There's a new client coming in that I want you to meet with. Her name is Vivian Kind. Her and her husband are divorcing, and she wants to sue the woman who would have been their surrogate. I'm not sure about all the details."

"Huh?" My brows furrowed.

"She'll be here in about fifteen minutes. We'll meet in the conference room."

And just like that he left. He wasn't the same charming man I met in Hawaii. I got up from my chair and walked over to the door, asking Colleen to come in.

"All you have to do is push this if you need me," she spoke as she showed me the intercom button on the phone sitting on my desk. "Also, here is the password for your computer."

"Thank you. What can you tell me about Mr. Wolfe?" I asked.

A sly grin crossed her face as she sat down in the chair across from my desk.

"He's so sexy, right?"

"Yeah. I guess." My brows furrowed. "He doesn't seem very friendly. Is he always like this with new associates?"

"No. Not usually. He's a huge flirt and a bit of a womanizer. I'm surprised he isn't being overly friendly with you." Her face twisted.

If she only knew about Hawaii.

"Wait until you meet his brothers." She placed her hand over her heart. "Ms. Wolfe knows how to produce beautiful children."

I wanted to tell her I'd already seen them and totally agreed. The Wolfe brothers were an eye candy distraction when they were all together.

"Elijah wasn't mean to you already. Was he?" she asked.

"No. I guess I just kind of expected him to be a little more friendly. But I'm sure his girlfriend is appreciative that he's not." I narrowed my eye.

"Elijah doesn't have a girlfriend. He never keeps a woman around long enough to establish that title. He likes to play the field and from what I hear, he gets bored easily."

"Is that so?" I arched my brow.

She leaned closer to my desk.

"Don't tell anyone I told you this, but his mother is the same way," she whispered.

"Interesting. Thank you, Colleen."

"Any time." She smiled.

"The client is here," Elijah spoke as he tapped on the doorframe and kept walking.

I sighed and rolled my eyes.

"Can you show me where the conference room is?" I asked Colleen.

"Follow me."

CHAPTER 13

*E*lijah

　　Aspen was already a distraction, and she'd only been here a half hour. The way her black tailored suit hugged her hourglass figure was unnerving. Usually the woman at the firm wore their skirts right above the knee. But not Aspen. Her skirt revealed more of her long lean legs than it should have. But who was I to complain?

"Hello, Vivian." I smiled as I extended my hand.

"Hello, Mr. Wolfe."

"This is Aspen Michaelson. She's one of our new associates."

"It's nice to meet you, Mrs. Kind." She smiled as she extended her hand.

"Please, call me Vivian."

The three of us took our seats at the table.

"So what brings you to Wolfe & Associates?" I asked.

"I want to sue the woman whom me and my husband hired to be our surrogate."

"Tell us why?" Aspen jumped in.

"My husband and I have been trying to have a baby for ten years. I soon found out I couldn't carry a child. We wanted one of our own, so we hired someone to carry our baby for us. That's when we found Melissa Marsh. She was smart, healthy, and she needed the money."

"May I ask how old Melissa is?" Aspen asked.

"She's twenty-nine."

"And you and your husband?" I asked.

"We're both thirty-seven. We spent a lot of time with her, invited her into our home and became friendly with her to make sure she was the right person to carry our child. We instantly became friends. On the day of IVF, we found out she was pregnant. She didn't even know it yet until the doctor told her. As you can imagine, my dreams were shattered."

"I'm not sure I understand why you're suing her," Aspen spoke. "Is it because she got pregnant while she was in agreement with you to carry your child?"

"I'm suing her because my husband is the father of her child. They were having an affair behind my back."

"Oh." Her eyes widened.

"Vivian, surrogacy contracts aren't enforceable in New York. So whatever arrangement you made with her is void," I spoke. "I would assume you contacted a lawyer for legal advice before you entered into the surrogacy agreement."

"We didn't go through a lawyer. We drafted our own private contract."

"Elijah is right about the surrogacy contract, but we can go after your husband for adultery in the divorce proceedings and we can go after Melissa for intentional infliction of emotional distress," Aspen spoke. "Adultery is still a crime in New York. We'll get the case in front of a jury and let them decide."

I shot her a look because there was no way this would hold up in court and I wouldn't be made a fool of.

"You said that Melissa needed the money, and that's why she agreed to become a surrogate for you. If you sue her and win, she has nothing to give you," I said.

"I'm aware, Mr. Wolfe. But if I win for what Aspen said, she will spend the rest of her life paying me. I will be a constant reminder of how she stole my husband and got pregnant with his child." Tears began to stream down her face.

"Vivian. The divorce is fine, and I can guarantee we can get you more assets in the division. Suing Melissa will be grueling and very expensive. It will cause even more stress for you," I said. "Do you really want to put yourself through all that?"

"Money isn't an option, Mr. Wolfe. I have plenty of it and will do whatever it takes to make the two of them pay for the pain and suffering they caused." She held out her wrists with the fresh scars. "A friend referred me to you because you're the best and I'm placing my trust in you."

"We will win this, Vivian." Aspen took hold of her hand from across the table.

"We require a retainer fee up front to get the paperwork started, and the case filed," I spoke.

"I can pay you the retainer fee right now."

"Aspen will start the paperwork for your case and hopefully we can get it before the judge within a couple of days," I said.

I stood up, shook Vivian's hand and the moment she walked out, I turned to Aspen.

"The testimonies of Vivian, her husband, and Melissa won't hold up in court. New York doesn't recognize the Alien of Affection Law. How could you sit there and promise that poor woman she'd win?"

"Because I will win this case. What happened to her was wrong."

"She tried to kill herself. Any jury will be quick to say she's mentally unstable. Not to mention the fact that going for intentional infliction of emotional distress is a one in a million shot."

"A one in a million shot I intend to win." I smiled.

I shook my head and walked out. There was no way this case would get past the judge and into the hands of a jury. I walked into my office and Marie followed behind.

"Well?" she asked.

"Well, what?"

"How did the meeting go?"

"Fine. Vivian is retaining us to file for a divorce and sue her husband's mistress for emotional distress." I took a seat behind my desk.

"The State of New York abolished the Alien of Affection Law."

"I know." I smirked. "Aspen seems to think we can get the mistress for intentional infliction of emotional distress and get it in front of a jury. It won't make it that far. The judge will throw the case out just like all the other cases that involve cheating. In fact, he may be pissed off at us for wasting his time."

"Then why didn't you tell Aspen that?" Marie's eye steadily narrowed at me.

"Let her find out for herself."

"You're setting her up to fail. Aren't you?"

"Your words, not mine." I smirked.

"What is wrong with you, Elijah? Are you still holding a grudge because she left in the middle of the night without a word?"

"No. She shouldn't be here period. I don't need the complication in my life. I have enough to deal with."

"What complication?"

"Her. We slept together, and we were never supposed to see each other again. Now that she's working here, she will expect more from me and it will make for an uncomfortable work environment."

She let out a laugh.

"So you think just because you two slept together she'll become this psychotic stalker and want more of you?"

"Yes." I arched my brow.

"It was one night, Elijah."

"It only takes one night. You see how the women I've been with behave."

She rolled her eyes and began walking out of my office.

"Your ego seriously needs deflating."

I smiled as she walked out and shut the door. I said nothing that wasn't the truth.

CHAPTER 14

$\mathcal{A}$spen

After Vivian left, I gave the file to Colleen and asked her to type up the paperwork.

"I'm heading to lunch. I'll be back in an hour." I smiled.

"Okay. Have fun."

I took the elevator down to the lobby and exited the building. My favorite deli was around the block, so I walked there to grab a sandwich.

"Hi, Aspen. You're back." Elie smiled from behind the counter.

"Hey, Elie. I am back and this time I'm not visiting. I moved here a couple days ago."

"Awesome!" He grinned. "Geneva has to be thrilled."

"She is. I'm working right around the corner at Wolfe & Associates, so you'll be seeing me around a lot."

"Damn girl. Wolfe & Associates? You're playing in the big leagues."

"I know." I grinned.

"Usual sandwich?" he asked.

"Yes. With a side salad and your house dressing."

"Coming right up. The sandwich and salad are on me today."

"Elie, I can't let you do that."

"Too bad, Aspen. Consider it a welcome to New York gift. Go grab a table and I'll bring it out to you."

"You're too sweet. Thank you." I smiled.

I walked over to a small table by the window and took a seat. Pulling out my phone, I had a voicemail from my mother.

"Hello, darling. Just calling to see how your first day at work is going. I'm heading out now and will be gone most of the day. I'll try to call you tonight."

As I placed my phone back in my purse, I heard the little bells above the door jingle. When I looked up, I saw Elijah walk in. Instantly, my belly started to flutter.

"I'll be with you in a moment," Elie said to him as he walked my sandwich and salad over to me. "Enjoy." He grinned.

"Thanks, Elie. You know I will."

After placing his order, Elijah tucked his hands in his pants pockets and walked over to where I was sitting.

"You're here one day and you're already getting special service from the owner."

"What are you talking about?"

"Your food. I saw him bring it over to you."

"Oh. I've known Elie for a couple of years. Whenever I would visit my sister, we would always come here."

"I see."

"Mr. Wolfe, your sandwich is ready," Elie spoke.

"I've been coming here for years and I still have to pick up my sandwich. I guess I'm not as special as you are."

"No. I guess you're not." I smirked.

He shot me a look, went to the counter, grabbed his sandwich and took a seat across from me. I didn't like his attitude.

"It is okay if I sit here, right?"

"You're already sitting, aren't you?" I stabbed my fork into the salad.

"I only have a few minutes. I have to be in court. For the Kind case, I'm letting you handle it and be first chair. Seeing as you're new to the firm, you have to start somewhere."

"That's fine." I smiled.

"You know that case will never make it to a jury."

"Sure it will."

"Ah. I see you're one of those delusional lawyers."

"I wouldn't say delusional, Elijah. I would say optimistic."

"How many cases did you lose back in Connecticut?"

"I don't lose." I cocked my head with an arch in my brow.

"Really? If you're as good as you say you are, Charlie never would have tried to move you somewhere else. If there's one thing I know, business comes before a wife."

"How would you know that? You're not married. Are you?" I raised my brow.

"No. Of course I'm not. Trust me. Business is the most important thing to a man. Business and making money."

"Hmm. I always thought the most important thing to a man was who he would put his cock in next."

"That too." He pointed at me with a sly grin.

"Charlie was thinking about his business when he decided he would move me. He was thinking about the millions he would have to fork over to his wife if she divorced his cheating ass."

He looked at his watch, took a sip of his water, and stood up.

"I have to be in court. I'll see you later."

Before I could respond, he flew out of the deli. Something was up with him. He acted as if he didn't like me. By the time I finished my lunch, I had about fifteen minutes left before I had to be back at the office, so I stopped at the pet store around the corner. Looking around, I saw the most stunning betta fish made up of bright fuchsia and deep purple.

"Hi there. Can I help you with anything?"

"I was just admiring the beauty of this betta fish." I smiled.

"She is gorgeous. Isn't she?"

"Her colors are so vibrant. I'll take her."

"Excellent. I'll get her bagged up for you. Do you have a bowl or a tank?"

"No, I don't."

"May I suggest this LED half-moon, 1.5-gallon tank? Or you could go with something bigger if you'd like."

"This will be perfect for my desk at the office."

While he was bagging up my fish, I picked out a couple of little plants for the tank and a bag of beautiful bright blue rocks for the bottom. After I paid, he handed me my bags, and I headed back to work.

"What's in the bag?" Colleen smiled as she followed me into my office.

I set the bag down on my desk, pulled out the fish and held her up.

"Oh my gosh, Aspen. That fish is beautiful. Does it have a name?"

"Fantasia." I grinned.

"I love it. I'll go get some water for the tank."

Once I set up the tank and Fantasia was in her new home, Colleen sat down in the chair across from my desk.

"I need to tell you something," she spoke.

"What is it?"

"You know the Kind case?"

"Yes."

"I heard that Elijah only took it on because he doesn't think you can win it."

"What?" I cocked my head in disbelief.

"I think he's setting you up to fail. To be honest, I don't know why he's acting like this towards you."

"I'm sure it has something to do with Hawaii," I blurted out by mistake.

"Hawaii?" Her brows furrowed.

I sighed as I leaned my head back in my chair.

"You're loyal to me, right?"

"Yes. That's why I told you about him." She smiled.

"So what I'm about to tell you stays between us. Understand?"

"Of course."

"Me and Elijah slept together in Hawaii. I didn't know who he was, and he didn't know who I was. It was one night, and I never thought I'd see him again. I didn't even know his last name."

"You slept with him?" Her eyes widened. "How did you leave it the next morning?"

"I left in the middle of the night while he was sleeping." I bit down on my bottom lip.

"That explains it." She slowly nodded her head.

"Explains what?"

"Why he's treating you the way he is. Elijah is a bit of a control freak and he's the one who does the leaving. I'm sure you bruised his overly big ego. Plus, he likes to hold grudges."

"Seriously?"

"Yeah. Seriously."

The phones started to ring, and Colleen went back to her desk. I couldn't believe he was setting me up to fail. If this was how he wanted to play, then game on. I'd show him.

CHAPTER 15

*E*lijah

I left the courthouse and walked back to the office. As I was walking past Aspen's office, I glanced inside and immediately stopped outside her door.

"Can I help you?" She looked up.

"What is that?" I pointed to her desk as I stepped inside.

"This is Fantasia. Isn't she beautiful?" She smiled.

"Why do you have a fish sitting on your desk?"

"Because it's relaxing to sit and watch. Especially if I'm feeling a little stressed or overwhelmed. I just take a moment and watch her swim around. It's peaceful."

"I see." I narrowed my eye at her.

"You should get one and see for yourself." The grin on her face widened. "You can borrow her if you want."

"No thanks. I'm good. Did you get the papers filed for the Kind case?"

"Yes. Colleen got in touch with the other lawyer and we're taking depositions tomorrow morning at ten."

"Were you not going to tell me?"

"I just found out a few minutes ago. I was going to tell you when you got back from court."

"Who is the defendant's attorney?"

"Lawrence Romeo."

"He's good. In fact, he's very good."

"I'm not worried." Her brow raised.

"You should be. I'll talk to you later."

I placed my hands in my pocket, and as I walked out of her office, I saw Colleen staring at me with a smirk on her face.

"What?" I asked her.

"Nothing." She quickly looked down at the papers sitting in front of her.

Rolling my eyes, I went back to my office. Pulling my phone out of my pocket, I noticed I had a text message from Mason in our group chat.

"Gym. Six o'clock. Don't be late."

"I'll be there, bro," Nathan replied.

"Me too."

&

We hit the gym and grabbed the only available bench. We usually met in the early morning, but Nathan didn't fly back until this afternoon. As Mason and I were loading the plates on the barbell, Nathan looked over and hit me on the arm.

"Bro, isn't that Aspen over there?"

I looked over and sure enough it was her. Damn it. My cock started to twitch as I stared at her fit body in her tight black leggings and hot pink sports bra. Her hair was up in a messy bun that sat on top of her head. Fuck my life, she looked way too sexy.

"Damn, Elijah. She is hot!" Mason said.

"And you have to work with that all day?" Nathan asked. "Shit. I'm not sure I'd get anything done."

"Knock it off."

"Who's that chick with her?" Mason asked.

"I don't know. Maybe her sister."

She turned around and noticed we were staring at her. Our eyes locked on each other's for a moment and then she came walking over.

"Hey, Elijah."

"Aspen. What are you doing here?"

"Working out."

"Hi. We haven't officially met yet. I'm Nathan and this is my brother Mason."

"It's nice to meet you both." She smiled as she shook both their hands. "This is my sister, Geneva."

"Nice to meet you." I extended my hand. "Are you a member here, Aspen?"

"I'm on a guest pass, but I think I'll join."

"Don't take this the wrong way, but you have some killer abs," Nathan said, and I almost knocked him to the ground.

"Thanks." The corners of her mouth curved upward. "It was nice to meet you guys. We're going to finish our workout and head home. I'll see you tomorrow, Elijah."

"Yeah. See you tomorrow."

Her and Geneva walked away, and I smacked Nathan's chest.

"Ouch. What was that for?"

"'You have some killer abs.' Seriously?"

"What? She does. I was complimenting her."

"Both of you keep your eyes to yourselves. Understand me?" I pointed at them.

Nathan rolled his eyes as he laid down on the bench and began doing some bench presses. I watched as Aspen picked up two thirty-pound dumbbells and took a seat on a bench in front of the mirror. She slowly lifted her arms above her head and started doing shoulder presses. Damn. I noticed the other men in the area eyeing her. They had the same dirty thoughts in their head as I had in mine.

"Elijah it's your turn," Mason said.

I laid down on the bench and did some presses. When I was finished, I looked over to find some guy talking to Aspen. He was smiling; she was smiling, and I didn't like it.

"You two finish up here. I need to talk to Aspen for a minute."

I walked over to her and the guy she was talking to looked at me.

"Excuse me, friend, I need to speak with her for a moment. It's work related, and I'm her boss." I arched my brow at him.

"Sure. Okay. I'll see you around, Aspen."

"Looking forward to it, Jake." She grinned. "What's up, Elijah?"

"I have a couple things to do in the morning. What time is the deposition again?"

"Ten o'clock."

"That's what I thought. Okay. I'll let you get back to your workout."

As soon as I started to walk away, Aspen called my name.

"Elijah?"

"Yeah." I turned around.

"Was that it? That's what you had to talk to me about?"

"Yeah. That was it. Like I said, I'll let you get back to your workout. But I hope you're prepared for the deposition tomorrow."

"I'll be prepared. Don't worry about it," she spoke with an attitude.

I walked away and headed back to the bench where my brothers were.

"What was that all about?" Nathan asked.

"Nothing. I just had to verify what time a deposition was tomorrow."

"And you couldn't just send her a text message later?" Mason asked.

"Looks to me like our brother didn't like another guy talking to his new employee." Nathan smirked.

"Shut the fuck up, bro. I could care less who talks to her. She's here, so I asked. What's the big deal?"

"Then you could have waited until they were done talking," Mason said.

"Don't you have a fire to put out or something?" I narrowed my eye at him.

Both Nathan and Mason started to laugh. Rolling my eyes, I laid down on the bench and began another round of presses.

CHAPTER 16

*A*spen

"I can see why you slept with him. If I wasn't married, I would have too." Geneva smirked. "He's yummy."

"Maybe on the outside, but on the inside he's a total asshole."

She stood there and stared at Elijah and his brothers.

"Will you stop staring at them?" I said as I put my weights away.

"I can't help it. They're all so sexy." She grinned.

I grabbed her arm and led her to the locker room.

"I have to go. I want to move the little things I have down to my apartment."

"When is the rest of your stuff coming?" she asked.

"In a few days. My furniture is coming tomorrow between one and four. I'm not sure what' I'm going to do. I don't think I'll be able to leave the office."

"Ask Lucas if he'll wait. I think he's working from home tomorrow."

$\mathcal{T}$he next morning, I stopped at Starbucks, grabbed my usual and headed to the office.

"Good morning, Colleen." I smiled as I walked into my office.

"Good morning."

"Good morning, Fantasia," I said as I set down my briefcase.

"You say good morning to the fish?" I heard Elijah's voice coming from the doorway.

I turned around and gave him a smile. Ugh. He looked so sexy.

"I do. She deserves a good morning just like everyone else. Good morning, Elijah."

He rolled his eyes and pursed his lips.

"There's a staff meeting in five minutes in the conference room."

"Okay. I'll be down in a second."

He walked away, and I flipped him off. Colleen saw and laughed as she walked into my office.

"Still not getting along?"

"He's an asshole." I sighed.

"But he's a sexy asshole." She smirked.

"I have a staff meeting to attend. I'll talk to you later. Can you feed Fantasia for me?"

"I sure can."

I walked down to the conference room and took a seat.

"Good morning, Aspen." Caitlin smiled.

"Good morning, Caitlin."

Elijah walked in, walked over to where I was sitting, and stood there with his arms folded.

"Can I help you?" I arched my brow as I looked up at him.

"This is my seat. You can sit in Harry's chair since he's no longer here."

"And where might Harry's chair be?" I spoke with a slight attitude.

"Right there." He pointed to the chair across from where I was sitting.

I gracefully got up, grabbed my notepad and walked to the other side of the table. Everyone was staring, and it made me slightly uncomfortable.

"Now that Elijah is here, let's get this meeting started," Caitlin spoke. "The Kind case belongs to Elijah and Aspen. Elijah, who is first chair?"

"Aspen will be first chair and I'll be second. We're taking depositions today at ten."

She glared at him for a moment before proceeding. "What's going on with the Quinn case?"

"We go to court in two days. This case is a slam dunk and it shouldn't take too much time."

"Excellent."

&

I was on the way back to my office when Colleen stopped me in the middle of the hallway.

"Aspen. There's a woman waiting for you in your office."

"Who is she?"

"I'm not sure. She came in and said she needed a lawyer ASAP."

"Okay." I smiled. "Thanks."

When I walked into my office, the lady with the shoulder-length brown hair turned and looked at me.

"Hi. I'm Aspen Michaelson." I smiled as I set my coffee cup down on my desk and extended my hand to her.

"I'm Renae Quinn. Thank you for meeting with me."

Quinn. Why did that name sound so familiar?

"What can I do for you?" I asked as I took a seat behind my desk.

"I need a new lawyer to represent me, and I know your firm is the best in New York."

"Okay. May I ask for what?"

"Malicious destruction of property."

"Did you have a previous lawyer?"

"I did and after our depositions, he dropped me. He said he doesn't want to go up against Mr. Wolfe."

"I see. What property did you destroy?" I asked.

"My husband's vintage guitar, his Lamborghini and his favorite painting worth 1.5 million dollars."

"Oh. That's a lot of damage."

"I recently found out he has a mistress. Some whore half his age he's been seeing for the past six months."

As I was writing everything down, my office door opened.

"Oh sorry. I didn't know you were—" Elijah stopped mid-sentence when Mrs. Quinn turned and looked at him. "Aspen, I need to speak with you for a moment. It's important."

"I'll be right back." I smiled at Mrs. Quinn.

Getting up from my seat, I met Elijah outside my office.

"What is she doing here?"

"Who?"

"Mrs. Quinn. That's my client's soon to be ex-wife that he's suing."

"Her lawyer dropped her after your depositions and now she wants me to represent her."

"No way. We can't. We're already representing her husband. You go back in there and tell her no," he spoke in an authoritative tone as he pointed his finger at me.

"And why is your client privileged enough to be represented by this firm?" I asked. "She has the same rights as he does."

"It's unethical, Aspen!" he shouted. "And a huge conflict of interest."

"Then we'll get them both to sign a conflict of interest waiver."

"No. No way!"

"You two in my office now!" Caitlin spoke as she walked past us.

Elijah walked away shaking his head, and I followed behind.

"What the hell is going on? I could hear you from the bathroom!"

"I'll tell you what's going on. Jonathan Quinn's wife wants to hire Aspen to represent her."

"We're already representing him," Caitlin spoke.

"Exactly. But Aspen doesn't seem to think it's an issue."

"Why should she get any less treatment than her husband?" I asked.

"Doesn't she have a lawyer?" Caitlin asked.

"He dropped her after the deposition with Elijah. He said he won't go up against him. She's entitled to have the best representation just like her husband. Why should she be penalized because other lawyers don't want to go up against him?" I pointed at Elijah.

"Are you really going to stand there and let her plead her case?" he asked.

"It's not a problem if they both sign a conflict of interest waiver," I calmly spoke.

She leaned up against her desk with her arms folded and stared at the both of us for a moment.

"If they both sign the waiver, Aspen can represent Mrs. Quinn," she spoke.

"You can't be serious!" Elijah spoke in anger.

"I am serious, Elijah. You both can leave now."

"I can't fucking believe this," Elijah mumbled as he stormed out of her office.

"Thank you, Caitlin."

"Don't thank me yet. Mr. Quinn may not sign. To be honest, Aspen, this is highly unethical. But you made a good point about Mrs. Quinn having the right to have the best representation possible. Be warned, Elijah will stop at nothing to make sure he wins, and things could get ugly."

"I'm not afraid of Elijah." I gave her a small smile and headed back to my office.

"Is everything okay?" Renae Quinn asked.

"I can represent you as long as you and Mr. Quinn both sign a conflict of interest waiver. To be honest, I'm not so sure he'll want to do that. You did destroy his prized possessions, and he may not want this firm representing you both."

"Excuse me, Aspen," Colleen spoke as she poked her head through the door. "Mr. Romeo cancelled the deposition for the Kind case."

"Why?"

"He says there's no need for one since there won't be any type of settlement. He said he'll see you in court."

"Thank you, Colleen. Call the clerk's office and see if we can get in front of the judge ASAP."

After Renae Quinn left, I walked over to Elijah's office.

"Hey," I spoke as I stood in the doorway.

"Come here to gloat?" he asked.

"No. Lawrence Romeo canceled the deposition for the Kind case."

"I'm not surprised," he spoke as he kept looking down at his notepad.

"You're not going to tell Mr. Quinn not to sign the waiver, are you?"

He set his pen down, leaned back in his chair and stared at me.

"No. If he wants to sign it, then that's his right. I will not influence his decision. But make no mistake, those two won't be the only ones battling it out in the courtroom. Are you prepared to lose?" His brow arched.

"Are you?" I asked as I turned and went back to my office.

Ugh, that man irritated me. How could I have been so stupid to have sex with him?

CHAPTER 17

*A*spen

My phone rang and Lucas was calling.

"Hey, you," I answered.

"Hey. I just wanted to let you know that your furniture arrived, and it looks great."

"Thanks, Lucas. I appreciate you waiting around for it."

"You're welcome, darling. Anytime."

I needed to use the bathroom. As I was walking past Elijah's office, I stopped and listened at the door that was slightly open when I heard my name mentioned.

"Who is this Aspen, and why haven't I heard of her before?" The man sitting in the seat across from Elijah's desk asked.

"She's a new associate, and yesterday was her first day at the firm. Listen, Jonathan, I honestly don't think you have anything to worry about. I'm not even sure she's all that good. Plus the trial is in two days and she knows nothing about the case."

"If she's not that good, then why did you hire her?"

"I didn't. My mother did. If I had a say I wouldn't have hired her at all."

That bastard.

I took in a deep breath and headed to the bathroom. Staring at myself in the mirror, I vowed I would not let the almighty Elijah Wolfe get to me. I had nothing to prove to him. I was a damn fantastic lawyer and everyone who knew me knew it.

When I went back to my office, Colleen followed me in.

"The clerk's office called."

"And?" I asked.

"You go in front of the judge tomorrow morning at nine o'clock for the Kind case." She smiled.

"Excellent. Can you let Elijah know for me?" I looked at my watch. "I'm leaving for the night."

"Of course. Have a good evening."

"You too." I smiled.

I grabbed the files from my desk and shoved them into my brief-case along with a couple of law books I needed.

When I arrived at my building, Donnie cheerfully held the door open for me.

"Good evening, Aspen. I see your furniture arrived today."

"Hi, Donnie. Yeah. I'm excited to get up to my apartment and see it."

I took the elevator up to my floor and stuck my key inside the lock. When I opened the door, I smiled as I saw the dining table and living room furniture sitting there. It was definitely starting to feel like home.

"Knock, knock," Geneva spoke as she opened the door. "Wow, look at this." She smiled.

"Do you like it?"

"I love it." She hooked her arm around me. "Come up for dinner. Lucas is making your favorite."

"Fettucine Alfredo?" I glanced over at her.

"Yep, and homemade honey rolls."

"I have to be in court tomorrow at nine and I have so much work to do."

"Well, you need to eat, and I know you don't have any food in here yet. So, come up, eat a quick dinner and then you can work."

"Okay." I grinned.

As we were eating dinner, I told Lucas and Geneva what I overheard Elijah say to his client.

"Sounds to me like he feels threatened by you," Lucas spoke.

"Why would he feel threatened?"

"Just from the little bit you've told me, it sounds like he's a control freak and you being here after sleeping with him is upsetting his balance."

"I don't get it?" I furrowed my brows as I picked up my glass.

"You slept together in Hawaii. You exchanged no information about yourselves except your first names. He was in control because he knew he'd never see you again. Then, you show up at his firm and his mother hired you without consulting him. His control is being compromised and the only way he can deal with it is by behaving in the manner he is towards you. The best thing you can do is ignore him."

"That's kind of hard to do when he's a walking sex god." I smirked. "But you're right. I think he is a control freak. At least that's what my secretary, Colleen, said about him."

I gave Lucas and Geneva a hug and thanked them for dinner. Sitting down on my brand-new comfy couch, I took the Kind file out, opened up a law book, and began working on my presentation for tomorrow. When I finished, I did some research on the Quinn case. I didn't have much time to prepare, so I needed to use my time wisely.

❦

I got up at five a.m. and hit the gym first before heading to the office. As I walked through the door, my eyes instantly diverted to the treadmill where all three of the Wolfe brothers were. Shit. I quickly looked away before they saw me and stared straight ahead as I made my way to the locker room.

"Aspen!" I heard someone yell my name.

When I turned around, I saw all three of them staring at me and only Nathan and Mason were waving. I gave a friendly wave and continued to the locker room. Making my way to the weight area, I found an open bench and began lifting some weights, trying not to notice the three of them heading my way. The only open bench was the one right next to me. *Please don't come over here. Please don't come over here.*

"Good morning." Mason smiled.

"Good morning."

"You're here awful early," Nathan said as Elijah picked up a weight and didn't even acknowledge my existence.

"So are the three of you." I smiled.

"We like to get our workouts in before the chaos of the day starts," Mason said.

"Me too."

"Well, have a good workout, Aspen."

"Thanks, Nathan. You too."

I continued my workout, stealing small glances in the mirror as Elijah did bicep curls. I kept thinking about that night and how his strong arms were wrapped around me. I gulped as I tightened my legs. No matter how mean or rude he was to me, I would never forget Hawaii, and I would never forget the man he was that night.

CHAPTER 18

*E*lijah

"You're being a dick, bro," Mason spoke.

"How am I being a dick?"

"By not even saying good morning to Aspen. You're acting like she doesn't even exist."

"Drop it, Mason."

"No. I won't. What is wrong with you? I've never seen you act so dickish before. I mean, you've always been a dick, but you took being one to a whole new level with Aspen."

"He's right, Elijah," Nathan spoke. "You want to know what I think? I think you like her, and you have ever since Hawaii, and you can't control it. Now that she's here, you're freaking the fuck out about it."

"You two are losers. I'll talk to you both later. I have to go home and get ready for work."

I went into the locker room and grabbed my bag. As I was heading out the door, I turned around to see if anyone was behind me. Sure enough, Aspen was in her short skirt and suit coat.

"Thank you," she spoke as I held the door open for her.

"You're welcome. You're heading to the office already?" I asked as we stepped onto the sidewalk.

"Yes. I have work to do before we go to court."

"I hope you're well prepared for this," I said.

"I am. I hope you are too."

"I don't need to be. I'm placing my trust in you."

I held up my hand, and a cab pulled up to the curb.

"Do you need a ride to the office?" I asked.

"No. I'll walk." She shot me a look and headed down the street.

"Lover's quarrel?" the cab driver asked as I climbed in.

"God no. She works for me."

"You're a lucky guy. I'd give anything to have a woman who looks like that work for me." He grinned.

I rolled my eyes and gave him my address.

ॐ

*L*ooking at my watch, it was eight thirty, and we needed to leave for the courthouse. As I approached Aspen's office, I could hear music coming from it. Slowly opening the door, I saw Colleen and Aspen dancing around the office.

"What the hell is going on in here?"

"We're dancing, Elijah." Colleen smiled. "Come join us."

"I will not. Turn that music off, Aspen. We have to go!"

She walked over and turned the music off.

"You need to loosen up." Colleen smirked as she walked out of the office.

"What is this? Why the hell are you dancing when we have to leave?"

"It's something I do to clear my head right before court. It helps to get me in the right mindset." She picked up her briefcase.

"You're weird. Oh my God, I can't believe this," I spoke as I walked out of her office.

We headed out the doors and walked to the courthouse.

"You know, Elijah, you shouldn't criticize what others do because it's not your thing."

"Excuse me?"

"You heard me. You think I'm weird because I dance. Maybe you're weird for not dancing."

"There's a place for dancing and the office isn't one of them."

"Says who?" she asked.

"It's just common sense, Aspen." I furrowed my brows at her.

We met Vivian outside the courtroom and standing across the way was Mr. Kind, and a woman I suspected was Melissa.

"Elijah," their lawyer, Lawrence Romeo, spoke.

"Lawrence." I gave him a slight nod.

"So you're the one who called off the deposition?" Aspen stepped up and asked.

"Yes. There will be no settlement negotiations. The deposition would have been a waste of both our times. I'm sorry, who are you?"

"Aspen Michaelson. I'm Vivian's attorney."

"It's time to go in," I spoke.

We entered the courtroom and took our seats. A few moments later, the bailiff walked over and told us that the judge wanted to see us in his chambers.

"Why does he want to see us?" Aspen asked.

"How the hell do I know. Probably to throw this damn case out before it even starts."

We walked into the judge's chambers and instantly, a smile crossed Aspen's lips.

"Aspen, sweetheart. How are you?" Judge Bloom got up from behind his desk, walked over to where she stood, and gave her a hug.

"I'm great, your Honor. Wow. I can't believe this. It's been a long time."

"Look at you. All grown up. I'm sorry about your father. He was an outstanding attorney."

"I thought Judge Hamilton was presiding," I spoke.

"He came down with the flu and the case was put on my docket.

When I saw Aspen's name, I couldn't believe it. You're living in New York now?" he asked her.

"I am. I just moved here. Since my father passed away, there was no reason for me to stay in Connecticut any longer."

"Well, I'm happy to have you in my courtroom and to see you in action. I know you'll be just as great as your father was."

As we headed back to the courtroom and took our seats, I looked over at her.

"I didn't know your father was a lawyer."

"How would you? You never bothered to get to know me."

"Maybe I would have if you wouldn't have snuck out of my hotel room in the middle of the night."

CHAPTER 19

*A*spen

"What did you say?" I asked him.

Before he could answer, Judge Bloom entered the courtroom, and the bailiff started to speak.

"All rise. Court is now in session. Honorable Judge Bloom is presiding."

"Good morning. You may be seated. In the case of Kind vs. Marsh. Are both sides ready?"

"Yes, your Honor," we all spoke.

"You may proceed, Miss Michaelson. It is still 'Miss', right?" He asked with a smile.

"Yes, your Honor." I graciously smiled back. "Mrs. Kind is suing Miss Marsh for intentional infliction of emotional stress and having an affair with her husband."

"Miss Michaelson, you know New York doesn't have an Alien of Affection law anymore, right?"

"I do, your Honor."

"Will counsel please step up to the bench?"

The three of us approached the bench and Judge Bloom looked directly at me.

"What is going on here, Miss Michaelson?"

"Mr. & Mrs. Kind hired Miss Marsh to be their surrogate for the baby she couldn't carry and then the two of them created their own child, causing Mrs. Kind a great deal of emotional distress to the point where she tried to commit suicide. Miss Marsh knew from the moment she met the Kind's that they had been trying for years to have a child. She knew that Mrs. Kind was suffering a great pain that she couldn't carry her own. So what does she do? Gets pregnant with her husband's child before the IVF was to take place."

"I object your, Honor," Lawrence spoke. "You cannot sue the mistress in the state of New York. I'm sorry, but this is a waste of everyone's time. My clients had an affair. It happens all the time. This is why New York doesn't have a law against this. The courts would be jammed packed with cases of cheating spouses every day. More than half the city would be in here."

"Miss Michaelson?" Judge Bloom looked at me.

"My client was both emotionally and psychologically harmed by the actions of Miss Marsh. She knew Mr. Kind was married, and she knew the emotional distress Mrs. Kind was going through not being able to carry a child. She acted in an intentional and reckless manner by sleeping with her husband and getting pregnant."

"Oh, come on," Lawrence spoke. "Like she planned to get pregnant."

"If two people don't use protection, it's a risk, and it's reckless."

"Your Honor?" He shook his head.

"Miss Michaelson has a point to some extent. I will place this in the hands of a jury. Date set one week from today. Court is adjourned."

"Yes!" I smiled as I looked at Elijah.

He didn't return my enthusiasm. I walked over to the table and Vivian hugged me.

"Thank you."

"Don't thank her yet. Now we have to convince a jury," Elijah spoke.

We walked out of the courthouse and headed back to the office.

"What did you mean when you said you would have gotten to know me if I hadn't snuck out in the middle of the night?"

"Nothing."

"Bullshit, Elijah." I grabbed his arm, and we stopped walking.

He looked at my hand on his arm and then back up at me. I let go, and we stood there on the street as people passed us by.

"Why did you leave, Aspen? I asked you to stay the night, and you said you would. Then I wake up the next morning and you were gone."

"Is that the reason you're treating me like shit? Because I left? We had sex, Elijah. That was all. What difference would it have made if I stayed? It's not like we would see each other again so why get all cozy and engage in some meaningful conversation."

He stood there for a moment and slowly nodded his head.

"You're right." He began to walk away.

"I'm sorry. Okay?" I walked with him. "Is that what you want to hear?"

"Sorry for what? Leaving or lying?"

"You act like I hurt you," I said.

"Ha." He chuckled. "Women don't hurt me, Aspen. I'm the one who does the hurting."

"Oh okay. Then I bruised your ego. A woman left in the middle of the night after having sex with the almighty Elijah Wolfe. Get over yourself."

We walked through the door of the building and took the elevator up in silence.

"Aren't you going to say anything?" I spoke as we stepped onto the marble floor of the law firm.

"No. You're not worth it, Miss Michaelson." He headed towards his office.

"You're an asshole, Elijah." I shouted down the hallway.

"I know and I won't apologize for it."

"UGH!"

"What on earth was that all about?" Colleen asked as she followed me into my office.

"Exactly what I said. He's an asshole!" I exclaimed as I sat down and laid my forehead on my desk.

"Change of subject then. How did it go in court?"

"The case is going in front of a jury one week from today," I spoke with my head still planted on my desk.

"Aspen, that's great news! Let's go celebrate at Rudy's after work."

CHAPTER 20

*E*lijah

    I slammed my briefcase down and fell into my chair, turning it around and staring out at the busy city. How dare she speak to me like that. I pulled my phone from my pocket and sent a group text message to my brothers.

"I need a few drinks. Can you meet me at Rudy's at seven?"

"I'll be there, but I have an early flight tomorrow so I can't stay late," Nathan replied.

"I'm off the next three days so I'll be there," Mason replied. *"Everything okay, bro?"*

"Just a very stressful day."

"How did it go?" my mother asked as she opened the door and stepped inside my office.

"The case is going in front of a jury one week from today."

"Excellent. She did it. Do you think you two can win the case?"

"Who the hell knows. I think I'm going to remove myself from the case and put Marty in second chair."

"Why would you do that, Elijah?"

"Because I don't want to work with her."

"Didn't I tell you to leave your ego out of the office?"

"This has nothing to do with my ego. She's just weird and rude. When I went to her office this morning to get her for court, she had music playing and was dancing around her office."

"Why?"

"Because she's a damn weirdo. That's why."

"So you're telling me she was just dancing around for the hell of it first thing in the morning?"

"She spewed some shit about it getting her in the right mindset before court and it helps clear her head. Do you believe that?"

"Well, everyone has their own way of clearing their head. It doesn't make her weird."

"Whatever, Mother." I rolled my eyes.

"Play nice in the sandbox, Elijah. You're staying on the Kind case. End of discussion." She turned on her heels and walked out.

I walked into Rudy's and looked around for a table. Instantly, my eyes caught sight of Aspen and Colleen. What the hell were they doing here?

"Hey, Elijah!" Colleen waved me over.

Shit.

I hesitantly walked over to where her and Aspen were sitting.

"Join us. We're celebrating the case going to a jury." Colleen grinned.

"No thanks. I'm meeting my brothers."

"Well, they can join us too." She gave a flirtatious smile.

"Maybe another time. They're here now." I walked away.

I couldn't even bear to look at Aspen after what transpired earlier. I walked across the bar and joined my brothers who just grabbed us a table.

"Usual boys?" Hanna smiled as she walked over.

"Yes." We all spoke in unison. "Make mine a double," I said.

"So, what stress was upon you today?" Nathan asked.

"Aspen. She got a case to go to a jury. I would have put money on it that the judge would have thrown it out."

"That's good. Isn't it?" Mason asked.

"The tough part will be convincing the jury to give our client what she wants. I don't think it's going to happen."

"Bro, she sounds like a good lawyer," Nathan said.

"She's a bitch. She told me today the reason she left in the middle of the night back in Hawaii was because we would never see each other again so why bother getting cozy and engage in a meaningful conversation. Can you believe that?"

As soon as Hanna set our drinks down, I picked up my glass and took a large sip.

"Okay? She has a point," Nathan spoke. "That's how I do it. Fuck them and leave. You do too, Elijah."

"Exactly!" I pointed at him. "I do."

Mason let out a sigh. "Just admit you like her, and you felt rejected when she left."

I steadily narrowed my eye at him.

"I do not in any way like that woman. She called me an asshole."

Nathan and Mason both laughed.

"You are one and you know it," Mason said.

"As are the two of you."

"Umm. Isn't that Aspen over there dancing with Colleen?" Nathan asked.

I turned my head and watched her as she danced around the dance floor. I rolled my eyes, threw my scotch down the back of my throat and called it a night.

"I have to go. I have court tomorrow and I need to be fully prepared."

"Is that the case where you're going up against Aspen?"

"Yep."

I walked out of the bar and stood at the curb, holding up my hand for a cab.

"Good night, Mr. Wolfe."

I turned around and saw Aspen start walking down the street.

"Where are you going?"

"Home."

"You're walking?"

"I just live a couple blocks away."

"Get a good night's sleep. You'll need it for tomorrow." I shouted.

She held up her hand and waved to me as she turned the corner. Ugh. That woman drove me crazy.

CHAPTER 21

$\mathcal{A}$spen

The next morning, as I was heading out of my apartment building, I stopped to talk to Donnie.

"Good morning, Donnie. Can you do me a favor?"

"Of course, Aspen, anything."

"My boxes from Connecticut are arriving today and I'll be in court most of the day. When the truck arrives, can you let them in my apartment and then lock up when they leave?"

"I'd be happy too. Good luck today." He smiled.

"Thanks. I'm going to need it." I gave him a smile back.

After stopping at Starbucks, I set my coffee down on my desk and fed Fantasia.

"Good morning." Colleen smiled as she walked in.

"Good morning."

"Are you ready to go up against Elijah today?"

"As ready as I'll ever be. I think." I bit down on my bottom lip.

"Well, good luck."

"Thanks. I'm going to need it."

I stared at myself in the mirror that hung on the wall in my office. This was going to be tough and with only a day and a half to prepare, I wasn't feeling very confident. In fact, the thought of going up against Elijah made me nervous. I took off my heels and began moving slowly to the beat, starting with my shoulders until I began to relax and let the rest of my body follow. Before I knew it, I was in full dance mode and everything else faded away. Until my office door opened and Elijah stood there with his arms folded and a look of disapproval on his face.

"Are you done yet?" he asked as he looked at his watch.

I turned off the music and looked at him with a smile on my face.

"I am."

Sitting down in the chair, I put on my heels, grabbed my briefcase, and we both headed out. As we were walking down the street, I told him about what I had overheard. I wanted him to know that I knew exactly what he thought of me.

"I overheard what you said to Mr. Quinn."

"What did you overhear?"

"That I'm probably not that good and he has nothing to worry about. Also, if you had a say, you wouldn't have hired me. I just wanted you to know I heard every word and I really don't give a damn what you think about me."

"Are you finished?" he asked.

"Yes."

"Good."

Asshole.

We stepped inside the courthouse. I met with my client and Elijah met with his. We walked into the courtroom and took our seats.

"You can do this, right?" Renae asked.

"I can do this. Don't worry." I placed my hand on her arm.

"Everyone rise. Court is now in session. Honorable Judge Swift is presiding."

We all stood up as the judge walked in. I looked over at the jury and studied each of their faces.

"Quinn vs. Quinn. Am I reading this right? Both attorneys work at the same firm?"

"Yes, your Honor," Elijah spoke.

"This is highly unusual. Did both parties sign a conflict of interest waiver?"

"Yes. They did, your Honor," I replied.

"Mr. Wolfe, it's nice to see you again. Did you enjoy your stay in the jail cell I put you in the last time you were in my courtroom?"

"It was an adventure, your Honor."

"Hopefully, I won't have to do it again. You may call your first witness."

Elijah called Mr. Quinn to the stand. Picking up my pen, I took notes and studied the reaction of the jury with each answer Mr. Quinn gave.

"No further questions, your Honor."

"Miss Michaelson, you may cross exam."

I got up from my seat and walked over to Mr. Quinn.

"Let me ask you something, Mr. Quinn. Did you really expect your wife of twenty-five years not to react when she found out you were having an affair?"

"Of course I did. I figured she'd scream, yell, and cry. I never thought she would destroy what she knew was so precious and valuable to me."

"Did you and your wife ever have any difficulties in your marriage prior to your affair?"

"Not really."

"Did the two of you argue?"

"Sometimes. But not very often."

"Did you ever hit her?"

"God no. I would never. I loved her."

"If you loved her, why did you seek the company of another woman?"

"OBJECTION, your Honor. Mr. Quinn's affair isn't on trial," Elijah stood up.

"Sustained."

"Would you say your marriage was a happy one?"

"Most of the time."

"Did you ever tell your wife when you weren't feeling happy with it?"

"No. I didn't. I didn't want to upset her."

"I see. You didn't want to upset her." I nodded my head. "Why? Were you afraid she'd do something terrible if you told her?"

"No. Like I said, I didn't want to hurt her feelings."

"Was your wife ever violent towards you or anyone else?"

"No. She wouldn't even kill a fly or a spider that was in the house. In fact, she would trap them and let them go outside."

"I see. So what Mrs. Quinn did to your belongings was very out of character for her?"

"OBJECTION!" Your Honor.

"Overruled. Sit down, Mr. Wolfe."

"Answer the question, Mr. Quinn, and remember you're under oath. Was it out of Mrs. Quinn's character to destroy your belongings?"

"Yes." He looked down.

"No further questions, your Honor."

I glanced over at Elijah as I walked back to my seat only to find him glaring at me. I called Mrs. Quinn and questioned her. Elijah badgered her. Things got ugly, and I threw a lot of objections his way. All of them sustained. He lived up to his reputation, and he was proud of it.

"We will resume this case Monday morning at nine o'clock. Court is adjourned," Judge Swift spoke.

CHAPTER 22

*E*lijah

She was damn good, and the jury related to her. I could tell by the way they watched her. I got up from my seat and followed Aspen out of the building.

"You're good," I spoke as we walked down the street.

"I know I am." She smirked. "Ready to drop the case?"

"Ha." I chucked. "No way. "But maybe I can talk to my client and see if he's willing to settle for a lesser amount."

"Denied. My client isn't paying a dime."

"Come on, Aspen. She should have to pay for what she did."

We walked through the doors of the building and she stopped in the middle of the lobby.

"The same could be said for your client."

"Why? Because he had an affair?"

"Yes." She walked to the elevator. "And I would think very carefully about the next words that will come out of your mouth."

"He shouldn't have to have his valuable possessions destroyed because he slept with another woman."

"And she shouldn't have her dignity and self-worth destroyed by a man she loved and devoted herself and her life to for twenty-five years."

She walked into her office and shut the door in my face. I looked over at Colleen, who was sitting there with a smirk.

"Don't you have work to do?" I furrowed my brows.

Walking into my office, Marie followed me inside.

"How did it go?"

"She's good." I sighed.

"Well, you already figured that out when she got the judge to take the Kind case to a jury."

"She's better than I thought. She might actually win this case, Marie." I glanced up at her.

"Whoa. Are you serious?"

"Yes. I'm very serious." I leaned back in my chair. "She smart and she thinks outside the box."

"That's good for the firm, right?"

"Yes. It is. Do me a favor. Call Charlie Connors in Connecticut and tell him that I need to meet with him tomorrow. Also, call Mario and see what time he can take me there in his helicopter."

"Why do you want to meet with Aspen's previous employer?"

"I need to find out exactly who I'm dealing with."

"Okay. I'll go call him now."

❧

I left my office around eight p.m. and went next door to Rudy's where I met Mason for a couple of drinks. When I got there, I saw Aspen sitting at a table with Colleen, her sister, Geneva, and a man I presumed was Geneva's husband.

"Bro, over here," I heard Mason shout.

I walked over to where he was sitting and sat down across from him.

"I already took the liberty to order your scotch." He smiled. "I figured you'd need it after court today. How did it go?"

"It went okay. She's great. I'm heading to Connecticut tomorrow to meet with her former boss, Charlie Connors," I spoke as I picked up my glass.

"Why?" His brows furrowed.

"Because I want to know more about her and her style of litigating. I already got a glimpse, but I know there's more to her."

"Then why don't you just ask her yourself? Take her to dinner and talk outside the office."

"Nah." I took a sip of my scotch.

"She sure seems to be having a good time," Mason spoke as he stared at the dance floor.

Turning around, I watched her as she danced with Colleen and her sister. She was jumping up and down, waving her hands in the air with a wide grin splayed across her face. Involuntarily, the corners of my mouth slightly curved upward. She was gorgeous, smart, and extremely independent. She was the type of person who didn't take shit from anyone but would let them know in a polite way. She danced in her office and kept a fish on her desk. As odd as I found her to be, I still thought she was the most beautiful woman my eyes had ever seen.

❧

"Charlie, thanks for meeting with me on a Saturday."

"No problem, Elijah. Have a seat. Can I get you a drink? I have scotch, bourbon, whiskey."

"Scotch would be great."

He walked over to his bar cart and poured us each a drink.

"So, to what do I owe the pleasure of this meeting?" he asked. "Do you have a case or something you need a consult on?"

"Ah, no. Actually, I want to talk to you about Aspen Michaelson."

Instantly, the color fell from his face.

"What about her? How do you know her?"

"She works for me at my firm."

"Are you married?" he asked.

"No."

93

"Good. Keep it that way. What about her?"

"Aside from what she did to you, I want to know about her litigation skills."

"She told you?"

"She was forced to by my mother. She's the one who hired her. Apparently, one of your associates in another department told her she stormed out your office one day and then abruptly quit."

He sighed. "Listen, the last thing I wanted to do was transfer Aspen out of this department. She's one of the best lawyers I've seen in a very long time. She brought in a lot of clients and she's won just about every case she tried. She's a master at settlements and she pulls out no stops in the courtroom. I just couldn't risk my wife leaving me and financially ruining me. I've spent my life building up this firm and making it what it is today. I'm not handing over half of it to my wife. If you were married, you'd understand."

"Maybe," I spoke. "So what you're saying is that Aspen will do whatever it takes to win a case? Ethically or unethically?"

"Yes. Don't let her beautiful exterior fool you. She may come across as this sweet and innocent woman, but on the inside, she's full of fire and she's fierce. She inherited that from her father, who was also an exceptional lawyer. And don't forget, she blackmailed me. She keeps quiet about her strategies. She only lets you know what she wants you to know."

"I see."

"May I ask why you want to know all of this?"

"I'm going up against her in a case."

"I'm confused. You said she works for you."

"Exactly. I have a client who is suing his wife for three million dollars. She destroyed some valuable and personal property of his worth two million and he's seeking the rest in emotional distress damages. His wife came to the firm and asked Aspen to represent her. Aspen convinced my mother to let her if both parties signed a waiver. At first it was no big deal because she only had about a day and a half to review and prep for court. Now, I think she may win the case."

"She probably will. Your best bet is to try and get it into settlement."

"I already tried. She said no."

"I'm not surprised. Aspen likes a good fight. I will tell you though that you're very lucky to have her. She will make your firm a lot of money. I'm already suffering the consequences of her leaving. But it's pennies to what I'd have to pay out if my wife divorced me."

CHAPTER 23

$\mathcal{A}$spen

    I spent the day unpacking and organizing my apartment. It felt good to put everything in their proper place. Lucas came down and hung my seventy-inch TV on the wall and a few other pictures I had. I stocked my refrigerator with fruit and vegetables and my cabinets with the staples. I was exhausted before night fell and I still had to work on a couple of cases.

I took a hot bath to relax and then I slipped into my comfy short robe. As I was in the kitchen making some tea, my lobby phone rang.

"Hey, Donnie."

"I'm sorry to disturb you, Aspen, but there's a Mr. Wolfe here to see you."

I furrowed my brows as a feeling of discomfort settled in my belly.

"Send him up."

The tea kettle started to whistle, so I walked over to the stove and turned it off. Suddenly, I heard a knock at the door. Opening it, Elijah stood there with his hands tucked tightly in his pants pockets as he eyed me from head to toe.

"Elijah."

"Aspen."

"How did you know where I lived?"

"I can find out anything. May I come in?"

"Why?" I narrowed my eye at him.

He sighed as he pushed past me.

"Okay then. Just come on in."

"Nice place you have here. How do you like it so far?"

"I like it a lot. It already feels like home."

"Good to hear. Two million."

"What?" I asked as I poured some hot water into my cup.

"Two million for my client. The exact amount of the damages. We'll forget about the emotional distress charges."

"We already discussed this, Elijah. My client is not paying your client a dime."

"I know what you're doing, Aspen." He paced around, waving his finger.

"What am I doing, Elijah?"

"You'll pull the temporary insanity card. You'll bring in some shrink to tell the jury that Mrs. Quinn was temporarily insane when she found out about her husband's mistress, blah, blah."

"And how do you know that?" I arched my brow at him.

"Because it's what I would do. Are you wearing anything under that robe?"

I took my hands and pulled it tighter.

"Why?"

"Just wondering because it looks like you aren't." His brow raised in a sexy way that made my legs tighten.

"Keep your eyes off my robe. Got it?"

"Sorry. It's kind of hard not to notice. Anyway, you won't budge. Will you?"

"Nope. Like I told you earlier, your cheating ass client deserved what he got."

"Fine. We'll continue to battle it out in court, and make no mistake, Miss Michaelson, it will get ugly." He pointed at me.

"Bring it on, Mr. Wolfe. Maybe other lawyers are afraid to go up against you, but I'm not."

He stood there and slowly shook his head as his eye steadily narrowed at me.

"Fine. We're done here." He began to walk towards the door.

"Yes. We are done here," I spoke as I stood with my arms folded.

He placed his hand on the doorknob and paused.

"Fuck it," he spoke as he turned around, walked over to where I stood and smashed his lips against mine.

I was shocked, but I welcomed it. I'd thought about those lips on mine ever since that night in Hawaii. This was so wrong, but I couldn't bring myself to stop him. I returned his kiss as our tongues tangled in the night. The kiss was hot and heavy, and he knew I wasn't going to stop him from doing whatever he wanted to. His fingers undid the tie to my robe, and he slid off my shoulders. My hands fumbled with each button on his shirt until it was undone and on the floor.

"I knew you weren't wearing anything under that robe," he mumbled.

His hands roamed up and down my body, gripping my ass before he swooped me in his arms and carried me to the bedroom. My skin was on fire and my body was reeling with excitement. He laid me on the bed and hovered over me as his tongue caressed my breasts in such a sensual way that I thought I was going to orgasm. He placed his hand between my legs and slowly moved it up until his fingers felt the wetness that poured from me. A moan escaped him as he dipped his finger inside me. I gasped at the pleasure and I became more intoxicated as he explored me.

"I'm not stopping until you come. Do you understand?"

"Yes," I moaned as I threw back my head, giving his lips access to my neck.

He found spots inside me I didn't know existed and sent me flying high as my body shook from the orgasm he gave me. My heart pounded out of my chest as I struggled to catch my breath. Climbing off the bed, he took down his pants and slipped on a condom.

"Get on all fours," he commanded.

Damn. The thought of him taking me from behind excited me even more.

I did as he said, and he thrust inside me. We both gasped and then let out pleasurable moans at the same time. His animalistic nature was hot. He moved in and out of me so hard that his balls hit my clit with each thrust, causing me to orgasm faster than I ever have. I let out a scream as my body fell from grace.

"Oh my God," he moaned. "That's it. God, I'm going to explode." His movement slowed as it was his turn to come.

I dropped onto the bed and he fell with me. The heat from our bodies collided as we lay there trying to catch our breath, and I felt the warmth of his lips press against my shoulder. He climbed off me and went into the bathroom to dispose of the condom. Rolling over, I sat up and slipped back into my robe. Now came the awkwardness of this whole situation.

He emerged from the bathroom and grabbed his pants from the floor.

"This can't happen again," he spoke.

"No. It can't." I looked up at him from the edge of the bed.

I stood up, walked into the living room, and grabbed a piece of paper from the Kind file. After handing it to him, he glanced at it.

"An updated witness list with the name Dr. Gregory Spiel. Surprise, surprise."

A smirk crossed my lips.

"I'll see you Monday," he spoke as he made his way to the door.

"If you would like to join me in my office for a quick dance session before court, you're welcome to." I smiled.

The corners of his mouth slightly curved upward as he opened the door and walked out. I slowly closed my eyes and took in a deep breath as I tried to extinguish the fire that still resided inside me.

CHAPTER 24

*E*lijah
      I walked out of her building and hailed a cab home. It shouldn't have happened, but it did. I couldn't control myself. Especially when I saw her standing there in nothing but that robe. The attraction to her was undeniable as was the sexual chemistry. But that's all it had to be. In fact, when I told her it couldn't happen again, I wasn't kidding. I meant it this time because I wasn't about to start something with her sexually and then have things become complicated when I couldn't give her anything more. She'd expect more. They always did.

❧

*T*he next day, we met for family dinner since we didn't on Thursday. We'd all be there since Nathan was flying back today and Mason didn't go back to work for a couple more days.

"Hi, Mom," I spoke as I walked into the kitchen and set the bottle of wine I brought down on the island.

"Hello, Elijah." She smiled as she kissed my cheek. "How is your weekend so far?"

"No complaints. Nathan and Mason aren't here yet?"

"Not yet. They both called and said they were on their way."

The smell of a roast cooking in the oven infiltrated the air.

"Do you need help with anything?" I asked.

"You can pour me a glass of that fine wine you brought." A smile crossed her lips. "How is the Quinn case going? Everything okay between you and Aspen?"

"She's good, Mom. Maybe a little too good."

"I knew she would be. She reminds me of her father."

"What?" I stopped pouring the wine and looked at her.

"I knew her father. We met twenty years ago in Connecticut when I attended a law conference he was a speaker at. When the conference was over, he asked me out for a drink. I accepted, and the drink turned into dinner. He was a wonderful man and one of the greatest lawyers I'd ever met."

"And?" I cautiously asked.

"If you're asking if we slept together, the answer is yes."

"Mother!" I exclaimed.

"Don't worry. He wasn't married."

"It was only one time, right?"

"No." A small smile framed her face. "We carried on our secret little rendezvous for almost a year."

"Jesus Christ. I can't believe this. How didn't I know?"

"I kept it from you boys."

"What happened between the two of you?"

"Eventually, he wanted to put our relationship out in the open and he wanted to meet you boys and he wanted me to meet his girls. The distance was hard for both of us, but he couldn't do it anymore."

"When did the two of you see each other?"

"Mostly on the weekends. Sometimes he would fly here on a weekday or I would fly there and then leave at night."

I stood there as memories filled my mind.

"Grandma watched us a lot on weekends. Is that when—"

"Yes. I told you boys that I had to go away on business. You didn't know any better. You were young. He wanted me to move to

Connecticut. I was just starting the firm, and it wasn't possible for me just to pack up and leave. Gabrielle said he understood, but I don't think he really did. He told me he loved me, and he wanted us to be a family. My career was at an all-time high and I wouldn't give it up, not for him or any other man. I had worked too damn hard, so I broke it off. But I never once stopped thinking about him. When I heard he passed away, the ache in my heart that had always been there resurfaced. When I saw Aspen's application come through, it thrilled me. He always talked about his girls, but mostly Aspen. He would tell me how she loved to argue, and that she would make a great lawyer one day."

"You planned to hire her before you even met her, didn't you?"

"Yes. I did."

"Wow. I can't believe this. And I can't believe you didn't tell me."

"We all have our secrets, Elijah."

"Hey, Mom. Hey, bro." Nathan smiled as him and Mason walked in.

"Hello, boys. Mason, set the table for me. Nathan, please take the roast out of the oven and Elijah, start cutting the bread."

After we ate, Nathan helped our mother clean up while Mason and I went into the living room where I poured us each a scotch.

"Did you go to Connecticut?" he asked.

"I did."

"And? Did you find out what you wanted to know?"

"I did. And now I know that I have to watch my back with her."

"She's that good?"

"Better." I shook my head as I threw back my scotch. "I went to her place last night when I got back to try and get her to settle. She refused, but that didn't stop me from—"

"No way, bro. You didn't."

"I did, and I told her it can't happen again."

"What did she say to that?"

"What did who say to what?" Nathan asked as he walked into the room.

"Elijah slept with Aspen again last night."

Nathan shrugged. "I knew it was only a matter of time. You're fucked, dude." He pointed at me.

"No. I'm not. We both agreed it wouldn't happen again, and if you tell Mom, I'll kill you."

"Oh yeah? Come on. Try it." He smirked.

I pushed up my sleeves and started walking towards him.

"Hey, you guys. Come on. Don't," Mason said.

I grabbed Nathan and threw him to the ground. We both started wrestling like we always did. Mason tried to break us up, but we pulled him in too. We got a little too rough as we hit the table and our mother's vase tumbled off and crashed to the ground.

"Shit," Nathan said as we all stopped.

"What the hell is going—" my mother said as she walked in. "Oh my God! Were you three wrestling again? I told you to do that outside! Now get up off the floor and clean this up. I want this vase replaced and you all have one week to find it and bring it to me!"

CHAPTER 25

*a*spen
    I stood in front of the mirror in my office and took in a deep breath. I still hadn't seen Elijah this morning, and it was going to be awkward considering what happened between us Saturday night. Today's case would end, and the jury would make their decision. I needed to be on top of my game because now, Elijah would pull out all the punches since I wouldn't settle. I picked up the remote, turned on some music, kicked off my heels, and began dancing. As soon as Colleen heard the music, she joined me. We danced, and we laughed. All the weight and worry of the case fell away and the anxiety I had felt earlier dissipated.

"For fuck sakes," Elijah said as he opened my office door. "This is so damn unprofessional."

I turned the music off and put on my heels.

"Feel ready now?" he asked with irritation.

"Yes." I smiled. "I'm ready to kick your ass in court."

"You wish," he spoke as he buttoned his suit coat.

As we walked down the street, I brought up Saturday night.

"Don't you think we should talk about Saturday night?"

"What about it?"

"The hot and amazing sex we had," I spoke.

"It was just sex, Aspen. Nothing else. Just like in Hawaii."

"But you said before that it would never happen again and look, it did."

"And you said the same thing. What happened to your office rule?" He glanced over at me.

"I couldn't stop thinking about the amazing orgasms you gave me in Hawaii. I guess I just wanted to experience it again."

I was so nonchalant about it that he stopped in front of the steps of the courthouse and stared at me.

"What did you say?"

"I'm pretty sure you heard me, Elijah."

"Good God." He shook his head and walked towards the door.

"And the way you were such an animal Saturday night. Hitting spots inside me I didn't even know existed. It feels like I can still feel your hard cock inside me."

I watched him as he swallowed hard and opened the door with one hand while the other was tucked tightly in his pants pocket.

"What the hell is wrong with you?" he asked as we walked inside.

"Nothing. I'm complimenting you. You are an amazing," I looked around, "fuck," I whispered in his ear.

Before he had time to react, Mr. Quinn walked over to him and I went inside the courtroom with a smile and met Renae. When Elijah walked in with his client and took his seat, I glanced over at him as he picked up his glass of water and guzzled it. I picked up my phone and sent him a text message.

"You should be proud of how easily you make me come, and how many times."

I glanced over at him as he read the message just as the bailiff walked in.

"All rise. Court is now in session. Honorable Judge Swift is presiding."

We all stood up, and I looked over at him again. A smile crossed my lips because he was flustered and now, he was off his game. I called Renae Quinn to the stand and began questioning her. When I finished, Elijah cross-examined.

"Objection, your Honor!" I stood up. "Mr. Wolfe is badgering the witness."

"Sustained."

"Objection! There is no relevance to his question!"

"Sustained."

"Objection, your Honor. Argumentative!"

"Sustained. Mr. Wolfe watch yourself," Judge Swift spoke.

He finished questioning her, and I called my next witness: Dr. Gregory Spiel. I questioned him, and when I was done, and when Elijah rose from his seat to cross-examine, I discreetly pushed my file folder off the table and onto the floor. Papers scattered everywhere. Elijah turned around and looked at me.

"I apologize, your Honor." I bent down to collect the papers and Elijah walked over and helped me. "Thank you." I smiled as I brushed my fingers against his.

He glared at me, stood up and started his cross-examination, in which he was stumbling with his questions. I sat there silently smiling.

"We'll hear closing arguments after lunch," Judge Swift spoke.

"May I speak to you in private for a moment?" Elijah lightly grabbed my arm.

"Sure. Renae, I'll meet you out in the lobby."

"What's up?" I asked with a smile.

"I know exactly what you did, and I can't believe I was so stupid to fall for it."

"What are you talking about?"

"The talk about Saturday night, the text message, the dropping of the papers and brushing your fingers against mine, it was to get me all wound up so I couldn't concentrate! You used sex to distract me from the case!" he spoke through gritted teeth.

"I would never do such a thing. I apologize for being honest about how great sex is with you."

"Keep your honesty to yourself from now on."

"Fine. I will," I spoke with an attitude.

"Good," he snapped as he walked away.

After lunch, it was time for closing arguments. Elijah closed first, and I watched the jury. The way they shifted in their seats and the expression on their faces. I wouldn't lie, his closing argument was good, but mine would be even better. I stood up from my seat, walked over to where the jury sat and presented my closing argument. When I finished, Judge Swift gave the jury instructions, and they left the courtroom. I glanced over at Elijah who refused to look at me. He knew my closing was exceptional.

"What happens now?" Renae asked.

"We wait for the jury to come back with a verdict."

I got up and went into the ladies' room. As I stood in front of the mirror, I stared at myself and took in a deep cleansing breath. I had to win. It wasn't an option. I just prayed to God that I convinced the jury to side with Mrs. Quinn. I also worried about what would happen between me and Elijah if he lost.

As I was walking out of the bathroom, Elijah emerged from the men's room and once again, I ran into him. Just like I did in Hawaii. I looked up from my phone as his hand held a light grip on my arm.

"Sorry. Why the hell do they have to have the bathrooms across from each other?"

"It's not the matter of where the restrooms are located, it's the matter of the person stepping outside of it to be paying attention instead of having her nose buried in her phone."

"Whatever." I rolled my eyes as I walked away.

"Your closing argument was good," he spoke as he followed behind.

"I know it was. I'd be worried if I were you."

Suddenly, both our phones dinged at the same time.

"Shit. The jury is back," I spoke.

"That sure as hell didn't take long. I'd be worried if I were you." He smirked as he held the door open to the courtroom for me.

"We'll see what happens." I raised my brow.

As soon as I sat down, Renae gripped my arm.

"They weren't out that long. That's a bad sign. Isn't it?"

"Not always," I sort of lied.

The fact that the jury came back so quickly had me worried.

"Will the defendant please rise? Foreman, has the jury reached a verdict?" Judge Swift asked.

"We have, your Honor."

"What say you?"

"In the case of Quinn vs. Quinn for malicious destruction of property, we the jury find in favor of the plaintiff."

My heart leapt into my throat.

"And we order the defendant to pay the plaintiff in the sum of one dollar."

I let out a breath as I looked at Renae.

"Oh, my God. Thank you, Aspen. Thank you so much." She hugged me tight.

"You're welcome. Congratulations." I smiled.

"Congratulations," Elijah spoke as he extended his hand.

"Thank you." I grinned.

CHAPTER 26

*E*lijah

"That little stunt you pulled was cleaver," I spoke as we walked down the street to the office.

She turned her head and looked at me with a sly grin across her lips.

"I'm sorry about that," she spoke.

"Never apologize for playing dirty in the courtroom. You did good, Aspen. My mother did right by bringing you into the firm."

"Thank you, Elijah. I appreciate you saying that. How's Mr. Quinn?"

"Pissed. He's ranting and raving that he'll fire us."

"He should know better than to underestimate a woman scorned," she said.

We took the elevator up to the offices. As soon as the doors opened, I saw my mother standing at the front desk. She turned her head and looked at the both of us.

"Well? How did it go?" she nervously asked.

Aspen looked at me.

"Go ahead. Tell her," I spoke.

"I won."

"Congratulations, Aspen. Great job. Elijah, how are you?"

"I'm fine. She presented a good case and delivered an exceptional closing. She had the jury in the palm of her hand."

"This calls for a celebration. Rudy's tonight at six o'clock," my mother spoke. "I'll go call your brothers and see if they can join us. Did you find my vase yet?" Her brow arched.

"I haven't had a chance to go shopping yet. Have I? You gave us a week."

"Just checking." She smirked as she walked away.

"Vase? What's that about?" Aspen asked.

"We were at our weekly family dinner last night. When me and my brothers were wrestling, we knocked over one of her vases and it shattered. Now, we have a week to replace it."

"Oh." She laughed as she stepped into her office.

❧

I went over to Rudy's around six-thirty and everyone was already there, including Nathan.

"Where's Mason?" I asked.

"He got called into the station. One of the guys is sick and in the hospital. I found it weird when Mom called and asked me to come celebrate Aspen's court win. How are you doing?"

"I'm good. You will never believe what the fuck she did."

"What?" Nathan asked.

"She used sex talk to distract me from the case."

"What?" He laughed. "What do you mean?"

"She kept bringing up Saturday night and what an animal I was and how she could still feel my cock inside her. Then she sent me a text message in court telling me how I should be proud about how many times I make her come. Do you fucking believe that? She set out to throw me off my game and it worked. It fucking worked."

"Jesus Christ, she's good. Shit." He laughed. "She really got you. I need to congratulate her."

I rolled my eyes.

"Go ahead. I'm getting a drink from the bar. I'll be over there in a minute."

"Hey, Elijah," Rudy, the bartender, and owner of the bar spoke. "Scotch?"

"Yeah. Make it a double."

"Coming right up." He smiled.

As I waited for my drink, a small smile crossed my lips when I turned around and looked at Aspen as she sat at the table. She was laughing and having a good time. Resisting her was becoming more difficult and now that we were working on the Kind case, we'd be putting in some long hours together. There was more than just a physical and sexual attraction. I found myself attracted to her mind and the urge to want to know her better grew every day. I was treading in dangerous territory and I needed to be careful.

"Here you go, Elijah."

"Thanks, Rudy," I spoke as I threw some cash on the bar.

I took my drink and walked over to the table, taking the open seat next to Nathan.

"Oh, I love this song!" Colleen exclaimed. "Come on, Aspen. Let's go dance." She grabbed her hand.

Nathan and I were talking when Marie walked over to the table.

"Who's that guy dancing with Aspen and Colleen?" she asked.

I looked over at the dance floor and narrowed my eye.

"Isn't that the dude she was talking to at the gym?" Nathan asked.

"Yep." I took a sip of my drink as I watched them.

A slow song began to play, and he hooked his arm around her waist and the two of them began dancing.

"Damn. He doesn't waste any time," Nathan spoke. "Looks to me like he's really into her."

"Marie, come on." I held out my hand.

"Seriously, Elijah?"

"Yes, seriously."

I led her to the dance floor, and I made sure we danced by Aspen and gym guy.

"Jake, isn't it?" I glanced over at him.

"Yeah. Aspen's boss, right?"

"You got it. Would you mind switching dance partners with me? I need to talk to Aspen about a case."

"Umm. Sure."

"I'm going to kill you," Marie whispered in my ear.

"You'll be fine," I spoke.

"What are you doing?" Aspen asked as we danced.

"You like that guy?"

"I don't really know him, but he seems nice. Why?"

"We need to sit down and discuss the Kind case. We're going to trial in a few days and I need to make sure we'll be ready."

"I thought you were leaving it in my hands?" she asked.

"I've decided I'm getting involved and we're working on it together."

"And you couldn't wait to tell me this in the morning?"

"No. We don't have time to waste, and I have other cases to work on. In fact, why don't we go back to the office and we can talk about it?"

"I left the file at home. I knew we'd be in court all day, and I planned to work on it tonight."

"Then I guess we're going back to your apartment."

CHAPTER 27

*A*spen
    On the way to my apartment, we stopped at a Chinese restaurant and got carry out since neither one of us had eaten since lunch. I was tired but Elijah was right; we needed to prepare for court and the sooner we got started, the better off we'd be.

We entered my apartment and Elijah set the bag on the island and began taking out the food while I grabbed two plates from the cabinet.

"We can eat while we work," he spoke.

"That's what I was thinking." I smiled.

I took the plates over to the table and then grabbed the file and opened it. We discussed the case and how I would present it to the jury while we ate.

"I think your strategy is good. But I'm not sure if it's good enough to convince the jury."

"It's good enough," I said as I took my plate over to the sink.

Elijah followed me with his and when I turned around, he was so close to me I was practically pinned to the counter.

"Here, I'll take that," I said as I grabbed the plate from his hand, turned around and set it in the sink.

My heart raced as the delicious smell of him infiltrated my space.

He needed to stop wearing that damn cologne. I could still feel him behind me, taking up the oxygen I needed to calm myself. I slowly turned around and our eyes met as I leaned against the sink.

"Is there something you needed?" I asked as I bit down on my lip.

"Is there something you need?" he asked as his finger swept across my lips.

I could feel the heat rise in my cheeks as the ache I already felt down below intensified.

"We made a promise to each other that what we both want wouldn't happen again."

"Yes, I agree." He slid his hand up my skirt and pushed my panties to the side. "But see, you're extremely wet and I'm already hard. Do you really think we should let either of those go to waste?" he spoke in a low and sensual voice. "I think we can break our promise this one time." His finger dipped inside me and I gasped.

I wrapped my hand around the back of his head and pulled him to me, smashing my mouth into his. I undid his belt and took down his pants as his finger explored every inch of me. Wrapping my hand around the shaft of his hard cock, I gave it a few tugs as moans escaped his lips. Within seconds, he gave me an orgasm. I cried out in pleasure as my body shook at the sensation. He quickly grabbed my shirt, lifted it over my head and then set me up on the counter. Instantly, my legs wrapped tightly around him as he wasted no time thrusting inside me with such force, it made my toes curl. Our lips found their way to each other while he moved in and out of me at such a rapid pace, we both came simultaneously.

"I know it's a little late to ask, but please tell me you're on birth control."

"I am. You can relax."

He let out a deep breath as he pulled out of me, pulled up his pants, and lifted me down from the counter.

"It's getting late. I better go," he spoke.

"Sure. Okay."

"You know what? I have time for one more drink. Maybe we can sit on the couch and you can tell me about yourself. We keep having sex and I really don't know a thing about you."

"I'd like that." I smiled.

"Great. Then go sit down and I'll pour us a glass of wine."

"I'm going to change into something more comfortable. I'll meet you on the couch."

He gave me a nod as I went into the bedroom and pulled on a pair of pajama bottoms and a tank top. When I walked into the living room, Elijah was already sitting down. He handed me a glass of wine as I sat down next to him.

"What do you want to know?" I asked.

"Anything you want to tell me. I already know you graduated from Yale with honors."

"Well, let's see. You know I have a sister. What you probably don't know is that she and Lucas live in this building a couple floors up."

"No. I didn't know that."

"We're very close. She's a couple years older than me. She got married and moved to New York a few years ago. My plan was to move here after I graduated law school, but then my dad got pancreatic cancer and I needed to stay and take care of him."

"That's understandable. What about your mom? You've never spoken of her."

"My mom left us when I was very young. Her and my father had their issues, but the issues were mainly her. She filed for divorce and then took off to go find herself. When she returned two years later, she had a boyfriend and thought she could just walk back into our lives as if she never left. I was angry and so was Geneva. We didn't welcome her back with open arms. What kind of mother leaves her two children behind for two years? It took many years to rebuild our relationship, but I never forgave her fully for leaving. Now she lives in California with her husband and they own an art gallery. He's an artist."

"I can relate. My father left us when I was four and right after Mason was born. He said he just couldn't do the father thing anymore. I barely remember him."

"You never saw him again?" I asked.

"No. He left New York and disappeared. My mother and my grandparents raised us."

"Your mom never remarried?"

"No. The day he left, she said that she would never be made a fool of again by another man. She's had her share of relationships over the years. But when the guy gets serious, she dumps him. What about your father? He never remarried?"

"No. He dated on and off but never got serious with anyone except some woman. I never met her. All I know is he deeply loved her, and she broke it off and his heart. After that, he gave up on finding someone to share his life with. But anyway, my favorite color is pink. My favorite food of all time is Mexican. You already know I love to dance for therapeutic reasons, and I love music. I also like to cook even though I never have a lot of time to do so."

"And you like to keep fish on your desk." He smirked.

"Yes. That too." I laughed. "Your turn. I already know you graduated from Harvard."

"And how do you know that?"

"I saw your diploma hanging on the wall in your office."

"Ah." He smiled.

"Favorite color?" I asked.

"Black."

"Boring. Favorite food?"

"Mexican."

A smile crossed my lips.

"Do you like to dance?"

"No."

"Weirdo. Do you like to play games?"

"Yes. In the bedroom." He winked.

"Somehow I knew you would say that," I spoke. "Do you like to cook?"

"Yes. Cooking to me is like what dancing is to you."

"Really?" I cocked my head.

"Yep."

"Then you must cook for me sometime."

"I definitely will." The corners of his mouth curved upward.

"How long was your last relationship?" I asked.

"Never had one."

"What?" I laughed. "You've never been in a relationship?"

"Nope. Sometimes I'll see the same woman for a while but it's just casual. Casual companionship is what I like to call it. If they try to tell me what to do or control me, they're done. If they start to fall in love, they're gone."

"Sounds like you have commitment issues."

"It's not an issue. It's the way I prefer things. I refuse to be tied down to anyone. The thought of committing yourself to someone isn't appealing. It causes too much chaos in a person's life and I don't have time for that. Look at the Quinn & Kind case for example. If everyone just stayed casual, they'd be a lot happier."

"Are you happy, Elijah?" I asked.

"Yes. I'm very happy. I have everything I could ask for. I have a great family, I'm successful and I have a lot of money. I can travel anywhere I want in the world and do whatever I want. Plus, getting women isn't a problem. Look at how easy it was to get you into bed in Hawaii." A smirk crossed his lips.

"Gee, thanks. Now you make me feel like a whore." I hit his arm. "Besides, you got lucky that night because I was down and vulnerable. If I wasn't down and vulnerable, I wouldn't have slept with you."

"Liar." He smiled.

He was right. I was a liar.

He brought his hand up to my cheek and softly stroked it.

"I really need to go. It's late."

"I know." I lightly smiled.

He leaned in and softly brushed his lips against mine. My insides still burned with desire for him and I found myself not wanting him to leave. Our kiss turned passionate. Passionate enough that we ended up in my bed, making love for the second time that night. When it was over, I cuddled into him, laying my head on his chest while his arm wrapped securely around me. Feelings crept up inside me. Unfamiliar feelings. I closed my eyes and fell asleep.

When I woke up, that feeling was gone and so was he. I picked up my phone from the nightstand and checked the time. It was three a.m. Asshole. I couldn't believe he left. This was his payback.

CHAPTER 28

*E*lijah

I waited until I knew she was asleep and then I left. Holding her in my arms after we had sex for the second time felt too good and when I closed my eyes, I saw us. Maybe it was just from the conversations we had earlier in the night. Who the hell knew? But the one thing I knew was that staying the night with her wasn't an option for me. I needed to get the hell out of there. I felt like I was drowning and the water that filled my lungs suffocated me.

I went home, stripped out of my clothes and climbed into bed. She would be pissed when she woke up and found that I had left. She should have expected it. I arrived at the firm around seven a.m. and when I passed by Aspen's office; I glanced through the window and just kept walking. I didn't know what to expect or what her reaction would be, but it was too early to find out for I hadn't had my coffee yet.

When I walked into the break room to grab a cup of coffee, I saw Aspen standing there.

"Good morning," I spoke. "You didn't stop at Starbucks this morning?"

"The line was too long," she spoke as she poured some coffee in her cup and walked away.

She was pissed. Just like I knew she'd be. After pouring some coffee, I grabbed my cup and headed to her office.

"We need to do more work on the Kind case."

"I did a lot of it already. I'll go over it with you later. I have a couple other cases to work on and I have a client coming in at ten."

"It's only eight-thirty. How long have you been here?"

"Since five-thirty," she spoke as she kept her nose buried in a law book.

"Oh. Couldn't sleep?" I cautiously asked.

"I slept great." She looked up at me with a smile. "I just don't want to fall behind."

"I see. Which client is coming in?"

"He's a new client. His wife passed away during a routine surgical procedure and he's suing the hospital. According to him, the doctor was intoxicated when he performed the surgery. So, if you'll excuse me, I have a lot of work to do before he gets here."

"Okay. I have to be in court at eleven, so plan on meeting later this afternoon."

"Sure," she spoke.

I walked away with an uneasy feeling. She was lying. She didn't sleep well at all. She couldn't sleep because she was pissed I left, hence the reason she was in the office so early. When I arrived back to my office, I saw Olivia sitting in the chair across from my desk.

"Olivia. To what do I owe the pleasure?"

"Hello, Elijah." She smiled. "My client will settle for the two hundred and fifty thousand dollars your client offered. I tried to get him to not take it, but he was adamant that he wants all this to go away. I think you scared him with that little stunt you pulled."

"Excellent." I grinned. "I will let my client know that we settled the case."

"How about dinner tonight?" she asked. "It's been a while."

Olivia Jude was one of my casuals. I hesitated for a moment and I wasn't sure why.

"Sure. I'll pick you up at seven."

"Great. I'm looking forward it." She smiled as she got up from her seat.

"I overheard that," Marie spoke as she walked into my office and set a file on my desk.

"Overheard what?"

"Your dinner plans tonight with Olivia."

"So?" I furrowed my brows.

"I just thought maybe you and Aspen—"

"Me and Aspen are coworkers. That's it. You should know better, Marie."

"I do, but I saw the way you danced with her last night and I saw something in your eyes. It's the way you look at her."

"Excuse me? I look at her like I look at every other beautiful woman."

"No, you don't." She smiled. "Keep kidding yourself. Even Nathan said something."

"Nathan doesn't know what the hell he's talking about and neither do you." I pointed at her. "What is this? Some kind of guilt trip?"

"Why would you feel guilty?" she asked.

"I don't feel guilty at all. I have no reason to."

"Obviously you do if you just asked if it was some kind of guilt trip. Why would that word even enter your mind?"

"You know what? You have work to do. Go do it!"

"Just saying." She pursed her lips as she walked out of my office.

§๑

*I*t was three o'clock when I arrived back to the office.

"Hey. I'm back from court. Are you ready to get back to work on the Kind case?" I asked Aspen.

"Sure. Just give me a second. I'll meet you in the conference room."

That was the first time I'd spoken to her since this morning. Hopefully she got over her attitude towards me. I grabbed a cup of coffee and went into the conference room. As I was looking at my phone, Aspen walked in, shut the door and sat in the seat across from me.

"How did your meeting go with your client this morning?" I asked.

"It went good. Depositions are tomorrow."

"Which hospital is he suing?"

"Mount Sinai and a Dr. Bernie Goodwin. Let's get working on the Kind case."

We did some work, and she seemed to be okay. I was just going to leave last night alone. She didn't bring it up, so I wasn't going to either. I didn't owe her any explanation as to why I left.

CHAPTER 29

*A*spen
    I wanted to strangle him for leaving last night. For disrupting my feelings of comfort and security. But what did I expect? He was Elijah Wolfe. Man whore, user and player. Just a man who had nothing but casual companions.

After work, I went home, changed my clothes and headed up to Geneva's apartment to fetch her and Lucas for dinner. We had reservations at Eleven Madison Park at seven thirty.

"What's wrong?" Geneva asked as we sat in the back of the cab.

"Nothing."

"Bullshit, Aspen. You know you can't hide anything from me."

"Really it's nothing. I just had a busy day."

She reached over and took hold of my hand.

"What's going on with you and Elijah?"

"Nothing is going on with me and Elijah. We work together. That's all."

We climbed out of the cab and entered the restaurant. As the hostess was leading us to our table, I saw Elijah and some woman sitting at a small table for two by the window. A feeling of sickness settled in the pit of my belly. But, like the nice and sometimes fake person I was, I walked over to their table with a smile on my face.

"Hello, Elijah."

I looked over at the attractive woman sitting across from him and instantly I hated her.

"Hi. I'm Aspen Michaelson. I work at Elijah's firm." I extended my hand to her.

"Olivia Jude. Nice to meet you, Aspen. Are you a lawyer there?"

"Yes. I just started last week."

"Exciting. How do you like it?"

"So far so good." I smiled.

"Gosh, I love your hair." She complimented me. "And your outfit."

She was being fake, and I could tell she felt threatened by me.

"Thank you. You're so sweet. Well, I better get back to my table. It was nice to meet you, Olivia. Elijah, I'll see you tomorrow."

"Umm. Yeah. I'll see you at the office."

"It was nice to meet you too, Aspen."

I confidently walked to my table and took a seat.

"Are you okay?" Geneva asked.

"I'm okay. Why wouldn't I be okay? I'm okay. In fact, I'm great. I don't care who he has dinner with. Why would I? It's not like we're dating or anything. Just because we had sex multiple times doesn't mean he can't see other people. In fact, the only thing he has are casual companions. Did you know that he's never been in a relationship? Ask me how I know? He told me last night after we had sex in my kitchen. He doesn't believe in relationship commitments. The thought of committing himself to one person isn't appealing." I rambled on at a fast pace.

"Aspen." Lucas placed his hand on mine and gently squeezed it.

I stopped talking and looked over at him.

"What?"

"Stop. It's obvious you're upset, and you just need to take in a deep breath."

"Okay. And honestly, I'm not upset, Lucas."

Was I upset? Of course I was. I thought maybe—oh, who the hell knew what I thought.

I ordered a bourbon and told the waitress to make it a double.

"Bourbon is a man's troubled drink, Aspen. It somehow always helps you see things a little clearer." My father used to say to me.

"She's pissed," Geneva said to Lucas. "She ordered a bourbon. Tell me what's going on?"

"Nothing. We have sex. We work together and have sex. I was lying in his arms last night and I don't know how to explain it, but I felt things."

"What kind of things?" Lucas asked. "Things you never felt before?"

"Yes. I felt safe and secure. Stupid, right? I think I just got caught up in the moment. We were talking about our family and I told him about Mom."

"I think you might be falling in love with him," Lucas spoke.

I picked up my glass and brought it to my lips.

"I can guarantee you I'm not falling in love with him. Anyway, he's totally not love worthy boyfriend material. He has issues."

"And so do you," Geneva spoke with an arch in her brow.

"Pish." I waved my hand. "I happen to like being in a relationship. You know I've had plenty of them."

"And you sabotaged them all," Geneva said.

"I did not. I was with Ron for a year." I pursed my lips.

"And you pushed him away, Aspen. Right into the arms of someone else."

"Thanks, sis." I narrowed my eye at her.

"It's true. Just when you get comfortable with someone you pull back and they end up leaving and then it's like you're relieved."

I sighed as I finished my drink. As we were eating, I tried not to look Elijah's way, but I couldn't help it.

"I see you looking at him," Geneva said.

"Am not."

"Are too."

"Both of you need to stop," Lucas said.

We finished our dinner and went back to our apartments. When we entered the building, Geneva hooked her arm around me.

"You know I love you, right?"

"Yes. I know. I love you too." I smiled.

"It's just that I worry about you sometimes. I want you to be happy."

"I am happy, sis."

"I'll talk to you tomorrow," she spoke as the elevator stopped on my floor.

"Thanks for dinner, Lucas. Next time it's my treat."

"You're welcome, darling. Stay out of trouble where Elijah is concerned." He smirked.

The first thing I did when I entered my apartment was kick off my shoes and turned on some music. I began dancing around the apartment, losing myself in my thoughts. I wouldn't be anyone's casual companion. Sex with Elijah was coming to an end.

CHAPTER 30

*E*lijah

I couldn't believe she was dining at the same restaurant. She was the last person I expected to see.

"She seems nice," Olivia spoke as she picked up her drink.

"She is."

"Is she a good lawyer?"

"Very good."

I kept my answers short and sweet.

"She's beautiful. Don't you think?"

"Yes. She is beautiful."

Her questions stopped, and I was grateful. I wasn't about to sit there and talk about Aspen with her. Nor would I talk about Olivia with Aspen tomorrow. We finished eating and as we walked out of the restaurant, Olivia turned around and grabbed the lapels of my coat.

"So, my place or yours?" She grinned as she brought her lips to mine.

God, she tempted me. But I couldn't get Aspen out of my head and it drove me nuts.

"As much as I'd love to, Olivia, I'll have to take a raincheck."

"Why? You've never taken a raincheck."

"I have this huge case I'm preparing for and I have to be in the office at the crack of dawn," I lied. "I'm sorry."

"Okay. But I'm holding you to that raincheck, and I want it soon."

I gave her a smile and hailed her a cab.

"I had a nice time," I spoke.

"Me too. Thanks for dinner. Keep in touch, Elijah," she said as she climbed into the back of the cab.

I gave her a nod and shut the door. Placing my hands in my coat pockets, I walked down the street for a while before catching a cab home.

The next morning, I hit the gym. Nathan was out of town again and Mason was working so I went alone. I prayed Aspen wasn't there. When I walked inside and checked in, I headed to the locker room and ran into her in the hallway.

"Hey." She smiled. "Good morning."

"Good morning. Did you just get here?"

"Yeah. I felt the need to get in a workout before heading to the office."

"Me too."

"Are you meeting your brothers here?"

"No. They're both working."

"Ah. Well, have a good workout." A smile crossed her lips.

"You too."

When I stepped into the weight area, I saw Aspen talking to the Jake guy again. What the fuck was his deal? He seemed to always be around, and it was pissing me off. I picked up some weights and began doing bicep curls. I watched them through the mirror as they stood and talked. She touched his arm and let out a laugh. I began to sweat as I did more bicep curls than I intended. He pulled out his phone and so did she. I would bet they were exchanging numbers. She smiled. He smiled and then he left. I could feel the rage inside me brewing as I laid down on the bench and did some presses. After I finished, I sat up, dropped the weights, and noticed she was gone. Looking around, I saw her heading to the locker room. I did a couple more presses and then called it a day. I couldn't concentrate.

๛

I walked down the hallway and as I passed by Aspen's office, I heard her say, "Did you have a good workout?"

I stopped in her doorway and stared at her as she sat there with a smile on her face.

"I did. You?"

"Yeah. It was good. Say good morning to Fantasia."

"Uh. No. One o'clock. My office for a meeting."

"Okay." She grinned.

I walked away more aggravated than I was before. Why the fuck was she so happy?

"How did your date go with Olivia last night?" Marie asked as she followed me into my office.

"It was fine," I spoke with irritation as I set my briefcase down.

"Just fine?"

"Aspen was at the restaurant last night with her sister-and-brother-in-law. She walked over to our table and introduced herself to Olivia."

"Busted!" She grinned.

"No. I wasn't busted. Why would you say that?" I snapped.

"And why are you in such a bad mood?"

"I don't know. I saw Aspen at the gym this morning and she was talking to that Jake douche and then I was walking past her office and she was all happy and shit."

"Sounds to me like you're jealous."

"Jealous of what?"

"Aspen and that Jake douche talking. Or maybe you're pissed that she isn't pissed when she saw you last night with Olivia."

"You're being ridiculous. I don't give a damn who she talks to. She's not my problem."

"Uh, huh." She slowly nodded her head.

"Get back to work."

"I am." She smiled as she headed towards the door. "By the way." She turned around. "For as long as I've worked for you and have known you, I've never seen you behave this way over a woman."

"Get out of here!" I shouted, and she laughed before shutting the door.

§&

I looked at my watch and it was ten minutes after one. Where the hell was she? Pushing the intercom button on my phone, I yelled at Marie to go find her.

"No need to yell. I'm here," Aspen spoke as she opened the door and stepped inside.

"I specifically told you one o'clock. You're ten minutes late."

"I'm sorry but I was on a conference call with the lawyer from Mount Sinai. They're coming in for depositions at three o'clock since we'll be in court all day tomorrow."

"Do you feel prepared for tomorrow? Fully prepared?" I asked.

"Yes. Do you?"

"Like I told you before, I'm trusting you. You're first chair. But I will warn you because of the nature of this case, I do not want this firm to be made a fool of."

"O-K-A-Y." Her eye steadily narrowed at me. "Why are you in a mood?"

"I'm not in a mood for fuck sakes. Why does everyone keep saying that?"

"Maybe because of the harsh tone in your voice?"

Suddenly my office door opened, and my mother walked in.

"Good, you're both here," she spoke as she took a seat next to Aspen. "Where are you on the hospital suit?" she asked her.

"They're coming in today for depositions."

"This is a huge case for you. Are you second chair, Elijah?"

"No. This is Aspen's case."

"Actually, Brad is second chair," Aspen spoke.

"I like Brad and all, but I'd prefer Elijah on it. Have you ever handled a case this big, Aspen?"

"No. I haven't."

"Okay, then it's settled. You and Elijah will handle it. I'll let Brad know."

"I have other cases I'm handling," I spoke in a harsh tone.

"First of all, Elijah, I don't like your tone, and second, you can handle it. No more arguments. I'm not in the mood today," she spoke as she walked out of my office.

I sighed as I threw my pen across my desk.

"Don't worry. I'll get them to settle. This case won't make it to court."

"A case this big and you think they're just going to settle for millions of dollars? They will do everything they can to prove there was no negligence and they will fight us right to the ground. This will go to court and to a jury."

"We'll see. Are we finished here? I have a few things to do before the depositions. I know you're busy so let me handle it."

"Go." I motioned with my hand.

CHAPTER 31

a spen

I ran into the building and fiercely pushed the button to the elevator. I was ten minutes late for my deposition, but it couldn't be helped. Once I stepped off the elevator, I ran to the conference room, opened the door, and walked in completely out of breath. Elijah sat there with his arms folded glaring at me.

"I'm so sorry I'm late. I apologize." I set my briefcase on the table. "Aspen Michaelson." I extended my hand.

"Will Owens," the nice-looking man in the expensive designer suit and salt and pepper hair spoke.

"Let's just cut right to the chase. Twenty million," I blurted out.

"Excuse me?" Mr. Owens asked.

"Twenty million for Dr. Goodwin's error and killing my client's wife while under the influence."

"You're crazy. My client wasn't under the influence. He is a renowned surgeon with many accolades, and he's honored every single year for his hospitable charity to the hospital. And you have no proof." He pointed at me. "It's all hearsay. Your client's word against my client's."

"I don't care if your client is the son of God himself. He was drinking and never should have been performing surgery."

"Like I said, you have no proof that he was drinking."

"My client smelled alcohol on his breath when Dr. Goodwin came out of surgery to tell him about his wife's death. This isn't the first time your client has been reprimanded for drinking on the job." I opened up my file. "Back in 2018, one of the scrub nurses noticed whiskey on his breath before he entered the surgical room, reported it to another doctor and they removed him from the surgery. Said doctor then reported it to the administration who slapped him on the wrist with a warning and warned the scrub nurse and the other doctor to keep quiet." I held up a piece of paper.

"How did you get that?"

"The only thing that matters is I did. I have nurses willing to testify that Dr. Goodwin seemed different the day of my client's wife surgery. He was unsure of himself and called for the wrong surgical tools twice by which the attending resident had to correct him."

"That was his last surgery from a forty-eight-hour shift," Mr. Owens spoke.

"Really? And that's an excuse? A patient died on his table. A perfectly healthy young woman. I also have testimonies from both of his ex-wives who stated he was teetering the line of alcoholism. There was also a complaint from a former patient who also said he smelled alcohol on his breath during a consultation. Thank God he had the sense to find another doctor."

"That's enough," Mr. Owens spoke.

"Mount Sinai takes great pride in having one of the top-rated urologists in the country such as Dr. Goodwin on their staff. People come from all over the country just to see him. Wouldn't it be a shame if this went public? The news reporters would have a field day especially since the hospital knew of Dr. Goodwin's alcohol problem. The hospital has done a good job already keeping this out of the public eye. If you want this to go to trial, then I'd be more than happy to accommodate you, Mr. Owens. Make no mistake. I will ruin the hospital's name and reputation along with Dr. Goodwin's. I will dig and dig until I find every mishap the hospital overlooked and chose to ignore, and I will make sure Dr. Goodwin never practices medicine again here or in any other state and country! Twenty million dollars to settle and this all quietly goes away."

"You're crazy!" He pointed at me. "Five million is all we'll offer."

"Elijah, don't you have a contact at the New York Times?" I asked as I glanced over at him.

"Yes. Yes I do." He grinned as he looked at Mr. Owens.

"Five million is an insult, Mr. Owens. Your hospital is responsible for the safety of their patients and they failed to keep Mrs. Larson safe while one of their doctors performed surgery on her under the influence." I leaned across the table and pointed my finger at him. "You can't ignore the evidence or the witness's testimonies. If the hospital would have properly punished Mr. Goodwin after the first offense, maybe this wouldn't have happened. But it's all about the fame for the hospital, isn't it? Well guess what, they'll really get their fame now."

"Can you excuse me for a moment?" he asked.

"Of course." I looked at my watch. "You have about fifteen minutes. I have another case I need to attend to."

He shot me a look and walked out of the conference room. I poured myself a glass of water and noticed Elijah staring at me.

"Damn. I think they're going to settle," he spoke.

"We'll see." I smirked.

Ten minutes later, Mr. Owens walked back into the conference room.

"Tell your client we're settling for twenty million. I'll draft up the settlement agreement," he spoke as he grabbed his briefcase and headed to the door.

"It was nice doing business with you Mr. Owens. Hopefully, I can have the pleasure again someday." I smiled.

He turned his head and shot me a dirty look before walking out.

"I'll be damned." Elijah smiled. "How did you get all that information so quickly?"

"I did a lot of work last night after dinner and a friend of my brother-in-law works in the administrative department at the hospital. He owed him a favor. I told you this wouldn't make it to court."

"You did great. How about we go to dinner tonight and celebrate?"

"Thanks, Elijah. But I have plans tonight."

"Oh. Okay. Another time then."

*E*lijah

She walked out of the conference room and I immediately picked up the phone and buzzed for Marie to come in.

"Yes?" she asked.

"I want you to find out what plans Aspen has for tonight. I want to know what she's doing and who she's going out with. Find out from Colleen. She knows everything that goes on with everyone in this firm. But be discreet about it. And try to hurry."

"Why do you want to know?"

"I just do. Now get moving."

I would guarantee she had plans with that Jake douche, and if she did, I would intercept. He wasn't right for her. There was something about him that didn't sit right with me.

I went back to my office and about fifteen minutes later, Marie walked in.

"Aspen is going on a date tonight with Jake."

"Thanks, Marie."

"What are you up to?" She narrowed her eye at me.

"I'm not up to anything. You may go now."

I walked down to Aspen's office and opened the door.

"Hey, I'm overly concerned about the case tomorrow, and I want every last detail you have. So, plan on working late tonight. We'll order something in for dinner."

"I told you I have plans tonight," she said.

"I know. I'm sorry but you'll have to cancel them."

"But you said—"

"I know what I said, Aspen. But I changed my mind. Conference room at six o'clock," I said as I shut the door and walked away.

CHAPTER 32

*a*spen

"Ugh!"

I picked up my phone and sent a text message to Jake.

"I'm sorry but I have to cancel our date for tonight. My pain in the ass boss needs me to stay to discuss a case we have for court tomorrow."

"That sucks. How about Friday night?"

"Friday will be good."

"Great. See you then."

Why the sudden change of mind about the case? What the hell was he up to?

At five fifty-five, I gathered up the files for the case and stepped into the conference room.

"Let's hurry and do this. I'm starving," Elijah spoke.

"You said we were ordering in."

"I changed my mind. I need to get out of the office. I thought we could do Mexican." He smirked.

"So you made me cancel my plans because you wanted to go over every detail of this case and now you changed your mind?" I cocked my head at him.

"Yes. And as your boss, I can do that."

I stood there and steadily narrowed my eye at him.

"What?"

"You did this on purpose because I wouldn't go out with you and celebrate tonight."

He sat there and shrugged, and a rage came over me.

"Here are the files. Go over them yourself." I threw them on the table and began to walk out.

"Have you forgotten that I'm your boss?"

"No. I haven't forgotten. But I will not stand by and accept this lack of respect from you! You had no right to do what you did."

"I have every right. You're my employee and there's work that needs to be done. If I say we're going over the case, then we're going over the case!" He stood up from his chair. "Work comes first, Aspen. Not your damn personal life. Whether you like it or not! Now sit down!" He commanded in a harsh tone.

"You, Elijah Wolfe, are an asshole!" I shouted back. "You've had it in for me ever since I came in for the interview. I have enough mind to sue your ass for sexual harassment."

"Oh, I'd like to see you try it, Miss Michaelson!"

"Don't underestimate me, Mr. Wolfe."

"I have a good mind to fire you for insubordination!"

I stood there for a moment in shock after he said that. Fine. If that's the way he felt.

"Let me save you the trouble, Mr. Wolfe. I quit!" I yelled and stormed out of the conference room.

I scurried to my office, threw on my coat, grabbed my purse and Fantasia and headed home.

જ

*E*lijah

"Shit," I said as I placed my hand on my forehead.

"I heard every word of that argument," Marie spoke as she walked into the conference room. "You're lucky I was the only one still here. What have you done, Elijah? Your mom is going to kill you."

Anger filled me. So much anger I couldn't see straight. God, what have I done? The thought of hurting her and making her cry gutted me. Fuck. I took in a couple deep breaths to calm myself down.

"I'll make it right," I calmly said to Marie.

"Your plan backfired, Elijah. Now look, she quit."

"I said I will make it right. I'm going to her apartment right now."

"Good luck with that. I'm sure she won't let you in. I wouldn't."

I shot her a look as I grabbed my coat and headed out. When I reached her building, I told the doorman I was there to see her.

"Sorry to bother you, Aspen, but Mr. Wolfe is here to see you." He looked at me with a strange expression on his face. "She told me to tell you that you're an egotistical asshole and you can go to hell."

I rolled my eyes and let out a sigh.

"Give me that," I said as I took the phone from him. "Aspen, I'm coming up to talk to you whether you like it or not."

I handed him back the phone and took the elevator up. When I reached her apartment, I started banging on the door. She had no choice but to open it or I'd continue banging.

"Open up, Aspen. I'd hate to keep disturbing your neighbors."

Suddenly, the door flew open, and she stood there with an angry look on her face.

"Thank you." I pushed past her.

"Go away, Elijah. I have nothing to say to you."

"Well, I have things I need to say and one of them being I'm sorry."

"And what exactly are you sorry for?"

She stood there with her hands on her hips looking sexy as fuck.

"I'm sorry for raising my voice and telling you that I should fire you. I didn't mean it, Aspen."

"Sit down," she said as she pointed to the couch.

"What?"

"I said sit down."

I walked over to the couch and took a seat while she stood there with her hands placed behind her back.

"Why did you make me cancel my plans for tonight?"

"Because I wanted to go over the case before tomorrow."

"But then you changed your mind, correct?"

"Sort of." I furrowed my brows at her.

"Yes or no? You were angry that I turned you down for dinner tonight."

For fuck sakes, she was putting me on trial.

"Not at first."

"Can you please clarify your answer?"

"I suspected that you were going out with that douchebag from the gym. When I found out it was true, I felt uneasy about it."

"And how did you find out about my date with Jake?"

"I had Marie find out from Colleen."

"So when you found out, you put a plan in motion to keep me from going. Correct?"

"Yes."

"And you threw in dinner at a Mexican place because you thought that would make you look better wanting to take me out for my favorite food?"

"No. I like Mexican, too. You know that."

"Mr. Wolfe, did you purposely and intentionally deceive me? Yes or no?"

I sat there and stared into her beautiful eyes.

"Yes."

"Why? Why would you do that?"

"Because I didn't want you going out with him. I wanted you to go with me. Okay? There, I said it." I stood up from the couch, walked over and gripped her hips. "I'm sorry. I truly am. Let me take you out and make it up to you."

"On a date?" Her brow raised.

I took in a deep breath. "Yes. On a date."

"Before I agree, you need to be honest with me about something."

"What?" I asked.

"Why did you leave the other night?"

Shit. I knew that question was coming.

"I don't know. Maybe I wanted you to know how it felt."

"Fair enough," she spoke.

CHAPTER 33

*A*spen

His damn cologne. It got me every time. How could I say no to a sexy man who smelled that good? We went out for dinner to an amazing Mexican restaurant that I deemed my new favorite spot. When he took me home, we wasted no time hitting the bedroom. The sex was as amazing as it always was, if not better. I climbed out of bed and went into the bathroom and started the water for a bath.

"What are you doing?" Elijah smiled as he stood naked in the doorway.

"Taking a bath. I was hoping you'd join me." I grinned. "I don't think I want you to leave just yet." I held out my hand.

"I'd like that." He placed his hand in mine and climbed into the tub first.

We lay there, in a bubbly hot tub. My back was against his strong chest as his arms wrapped securely around me.

"I'm sorry if I made you cry earlier," he spoke.

"You didn't make me cry. Why would you think I cried?"

"Because I yelled at you? I don't know. I just figured you were so upset, you cried."

"I don't cry." I softly stroked his arm.

"What do you mean you don't cry?"

"I haven't cried a single tear since I was a child."

"Not even at your father's funeral?"

"No."

"Not even when your boyfriend broke up with you?"

"No." I tilted my head back and looked up at him.

"Is there something wrong with you?"

I let out a light laugh.

"According to Lucas, my brother-in-law the psychiatrist, the trauma from my mother leaving has prevented the tears from ever flowing again."

"I don't think I understand."

"The last time I cried was when she left us. I remember her walking out the door with her suitcases and I went running after her. I was sobbing as I pulled on her coat, begging her not to leave. I never cried so hard before and I never felt my heart break like it did. That night as I was lying in bed with Geneva, the tears just suddenly stopped, and I never cried a single tear again. Lucas said that I won't allow myself to feel that kind of pain again."

"I think I can understand that," he spoke as he kissed the top of my head. "I'm sorry you had to go through that. I barely remember when my dad left. I suppose I blocked it out of my memory. I know it's late, but would you mind if I stayed the night? I can get up early and go back to my place to shower and get fresh clothes."

"I'd love for you to stay the night." I smiled. "But, if I wake up and you're gone, it won't be pretty."

He let out a chuckle. "I promise I won't sneak out, and you're not quitting. I won't have it. Do you understand me?"

"I understand you, Mr. Wolfe."

"Good." He smiled.

*T*he next morning, the alarm went off at five a.m. When I opened my eyes, I smiled as I felt Elijah's arm tightly wrapped around me and the feel of his lips pressed against the back of my head.

"Good morning." I turned around and faced him.

"Good morning."

"You stayed."

"I told you I would." He tenderly kissed my lips.

"Would you like some coffee before you go?"

"That would be great."

I climbed out of bed and slipped into my robe. Walking into the kitchen, I said good morning to Fantasia and then popped a K-cup in the Keurig and waited for his coffee to brew. He came up from behind and wrapped his arms around me.

"Say good morning to Fantasia," I spoke as I turned around in his arms.

"No." He kissed my lips.

I removed the coffee cup from the brewer and held it up in the air.

"Say good morning to Fantasia or else you don't get this amazing smelling coffee."

"You're going to spill that and burn yourself," he spoke.

"If you want it, you need to show some respect to the fish." I grinned.

"Come on, Aspen." He reached for the cup and I took a few steps back.

"Tell Fantasia good morning."

"Fine." He walked over to where I had her sitting on the island. "Good morning, Fantasia."

"Thank you." I smiled as I handed him his coffee.

He took it into the bedroom and slipped into his clothes, while I stood there with my cup and watched him.

"Thank you for the coffee." He kissed me. "I have to get home. I'll see you soon."

"You're welcome. I'll see you at the office."

As soon as he left, I jumped in the shower and ran my hands along my body. I could still feel the lingering effects of the six orgasms he gave me during our three-time sex fest last night. There was no doubt in my mind that the emotions I felt when I was with him was love. For the first time in my life I was falling in love and it scared the hell out of me.

CHAPTER 34

*E*lijah

Last night was indescribable. The overwhelming feelings that soared through me were a bit unsettling while they took me over. They took me over in such a way that it began to freak me the hell out.

Walking into my office, Marie jumped up and followed me in.

"I saw Aspen is here. Good job in smoothing things over. How did you get her to forgive you?" She smirked.

"And what did Aspen need to forgive you for?" my mother asked as she walked in.

"Good morning, Ms.. Wolfe," Marie spoke as she walked out and shut the door.

"What did you do, Elijah?"

"Nothing, Mother. We just had a disagreement. That's all."

"You're lying, my darling son. Is this still about her sneaking out on you back in Hawaii?"

"No. I'm over that. We just had a disagreement about the Kind case. I said some things I shouldn't have, and I apologized. It's all good now."

"Okay." She gave me that stern mother look. "I'm impressed with her and if she keeps going the way she is, she may just make partner. The way she got that hospital to settle without even stepping foot in a courtroom was very admirable. Not to mention that she also beat you in court." She smirked.

"Yeah. Yeah." I waved my hand. "Was there anything else? I need to get to court."

"Don't forget family dinner is tonight. I expect you at seven o'clock."

"You know I'll be there." I smiled.

I grabbed my coat and my briefcase and walked down to Aspen's office. As I approached her door, I could already hear the music playing. Opening the door, I smiled as I saw her dancing around. Instead of bothering her like I always do, I shut the door and waited for her to finish.

"You're getting used to her doing that." Colleen smiled.

"Yeah. Maybe I am," I spoke as I leaned up against her desk with my hands in my pockets.

Suddenly, the music stopped, the door opened, and Aspen stood there holding her briefcase in her hand.

"Are you ready now?" I smiled.

"I am. Are you?"

"Let's do this."

✥

*A*spen
"You knew the struggle and depression Mrs. Kind was going through trying to have a baby," I shouted. "She turned to you for help in fulfilling her dream and what did you do?!"

"Objection, your Honor! She's badgering the witness."

"Sustained."

"You slept with her husband!"

"Your Honor, Objection!"

"And not only did you sleep with him, you got pregnant!"

"OBJECTION!"

"Sustained. I'm warning you, Miss Michaelson."

"The one thing Mrs. Kind wanted the most with her husband and you stole it!"

"OBJECTION!" Opposing counsel stood up and slammed his fist on the table.

"SUSTAINED!"

"No more questions, your Honor."

"Miss Michaelson, in my chambers now!"

I sighed as the bailiff escorted me and Elijah into Judge Bloom's chambers.

"Good job." Elijah smiled. "I'll bail you out of jail. Don't worry."

"Thanks. I appreciate that."

"Miss Michaelson, I will not tolerate that type of behavior in my courtroom. Do you understand me?"

"Yes, your Honor. I apologize."

"This is your one and only warning. If you present that behavior in my courtroom again, I will have no choice but to hold you in contempt."

"I'm sorry, your Honor. It won't happen again."

"Everyone back in the courtroom," he spoke.

*C*ourt had ended for the day, so we headed back to the office. So far, I was pleased with the way the trial was going.

"You had the jury." Elijah smiled as we walked down the street.

"You think?"

"I was watching their reactions when you were cross-examining Melissa."

"Just wait until I cross-examine, Mr. Kind." I smirked.

"I got to thinking and you've never been to my penthouse."

"No. I haven't."

"How about I cook dinner for you tomorrow night?"

"I'd like that." I smiled at him.

"Good. I'll text you my address." A sexy grin crossed his lips.

When we arrived at the building, we took the elevator up and he went to his office and I went to mine. I was happy. Not only because the case was going well, but because Elijah was cooking dinner for me. Shit! It had just hit me that I had made plans with Jake for tomorrow night. Ugh. Pulling out my phone, I sent him a text message.

"Hi. I'm so sorry to have to do this, but I need to cancel for tomorrow night. I totally forgot I had dinner plans with my sister."

I know. I know. I lied. But I couldn't tell him I was cancelling our date to be with another guy.

"Hey. That's okay. It seems like you're busy all the time. I really wanted to go out with you, but I think you just might be a little too busy for my liking. See you around, Aspen."

I sat there and read his message with furrowed brows. What the hell? Maybe Elijah was right in calling him a douche.

CHAPTER 35

*E*lijah

I walked into my mother's townhouse and found Nathan and Mason sitting in the living room.

"What are you two doing? Why aren't you helping Mom in the kitchen?"

"Mom's not home yet," Nathan spoke.

"Where is she? She left the office a couple hours ago."

"I don't know. I sent her a text, and she said she'd be home in about fifteen minutes." He looked at his watch. "That was fifteen minutes ago."

As I walked over to the bar to pour a drink, the front door opened, and my mother walked in carrying two large bags. Mason and Nathan jumped up from the couch and grabbed them from her.

"Sorry I'm late," she spoke as I followed her into the kitchen. "I stopped on the way home and got us a carry out from that cute little Thai place around the corner."

"No home cooked meal tonight, Mom?" Mason pouted.

"Not tonight, darling."

She took off her coat, and I noticed the buttoning on her blouse was wrong.

"So, where were you?" I asked as I grabbed the plates from the cabinet.

"I had some errands to run."

"Really? I don't see any bags besides the food. What errands? You left the office over two hours ago."

"I said I had errands, Elijah. Can you please pour me a glass of wine? I'm going upstairs to change."

"I will. But not until you answer my question. Who were you with?"

She stopped in the middle of the kitchen, turned around and stared at me.

"What makes you think I was with someone?" she asked.

"The evidence." I pointed to her blouse.

She looked down.

"Mom, come on," Nathan said.

"Yeah, Mom. Gross," Mason chimed in.

She sighed and rolled her eyes.

"If the three of you must know, I was with Tommy McNeil."

"District Attorney McNeil?" I asked in shock.

"Mom, isn't he like twenty years younger than you?" Mason asked.

"Go, Mom!" Nathan smiled.

"Age doesn't matter when you get to be my age. I don't want to discuss it. I'll be down in a minute. Start eating before the food gets cold."

"I think I suddenly lost my appetite," Mason said.

I smacked him on the back of the head.

"Go sit down."

The three of us took our seats and began eating.

"Our mother is a cougar," Nathan said.

"Forget the cougar part. She's sleeping with the district attorney. Shit," I spoke.

"Are you finished talking about me?" she asked as she walked into the dining room. "I have needs just like you boys do. Do I question your sex life? Do I question how all three of you are playboys and sleep with any woman who looks your way?"

"That is not true," Mason said.

"I guess the apple doesn't fall far from the tree." Nathan smirked.

"Tommy and I have been seeing each other on and off for a while. But we're keeping it on the down low. So don't you boys mention it to anyone."

"And how long is a while?" I asked.

"A couple of months."

"And you couldn't tell us, why?"

"Do I ask you every week who you're sleeping with?" She smiled. "Now, let's change the subject. How was court today?"

"It was good. We should be able to wrap up tomorrow and present closing arguments on Monday. You should have seen Aspen." I smiled. "The judge called her in his chambers and gave her a warning. I honestly didn't think she was going to stop."

"I love the way your eyes light up when you talk about sweet Aspen." Nathan grinned.

"Shut the fuck up, bro!"

"That's enough, Nathan. Elijah, watch your language."

After we finished eating, we had dessert and a couple of drinks and then called it a night. Me, Nathan and Mason all left together.

"So what's going on with you and Aspen?" Mason asked.

"We're friends with benefits." I smirked.

"Until she falls in love with you," Nathan spoke. "Or vice versa."

"The three of us are incapable of love," Mason said.

"True," Nathan said.

"I will not fall in love with her. I've been with a lot of women and have I ever?" I asked.

"No. But there's a first time for everything." Nathan smiled.

"Trust me. If I even see a hint of her falling in love with me, it's over. Just like all the rest."

"But won't that make it awkward at the office?" Mason asked.

"I'll deal with it."

CHAPTER 36

Aspen

"Miss Marsh, how many times did you and Mr. Kind use a condom?"

"We didn't have to. I had an IUD."

"Did you have the IUD in when you went for the IVF appointment?"

"No. I had it taken out five days before."

"Did you and Mr. Kind have sex after it was taken out?"

"No."

"Do you recall the date you had your doctor's appointment to have the IUD removed?"

"I believe it was August 1st."

"I have a copy of your OB/GYN's appointment log for the entire month of August and it shows you never had an appointment."

"Maybe I was mistaken about the date and it was July 31st."

"No." I shook my head. "You didn't have an appointment in July either. In fact, according to your doctor's records, the last time you were at his office was over a year ago."

"They probably made a mistake. I was there."

"How many times have you been pregnant?"

"Objection, your Honor!"

"Let me rephrase the question. Is this your first pregnancy? And remember you're under oath."

"No. It isn't. I had a miscarriage two years ago."

"And who was the father of that child?"

"Objection, your Honor. Relevance?"

"I promise, your Honor. I am going somewhere with this."

"You better be, Miss Michaelson. Overruled."

"Just a guy."

"A guy named Ben Carraway, perhaps?"

"Yeah. He was my boyfriend."

"He was also Jean Carraway's husband. Did you know her? Again, you're under oath. And in case you didn't know, perjury is a crime and punishable up to seven years in prison."

"Yes. I knew her."

"Please tell the jury how you knew her."

She hesitated.

"Miss Marsh, answer the question," Judge Bloom spoke.

"She hired me to be their surrogate."

"Let me get this straight. The Carraway's hired you to be their surrogate just like the Kind's did. They trusted you enough to want you to carry their child for them and you slept with both husbands using no protection at all and got pregnant by both men. I see a pattern here, Miss Marsh."

"Objection, your Honor. Speculation!"

"How is that speculation, Counsel? You just heard the testimony from your client. Overruled."

"You were never on birth control, were you?"

She sat there as tears streamed down her face and hesitated.

"Answer the question, Miss Marsh."

"No."

"So you lied to Mr. Kind about having an IUD?"

"Yes," she cried.

"No further questions."

As I walked back to the table, Elijah winked at me.

"Court is adjourned for today. We will resume Monday morning and hear closing arguments."

§∎

*E*lijah lived on One West End on the Upper West Side in a beautiful sculptural glass high rise. Taking the elevator up the thirtieth floor, I knocked on the door of Penthouse B.

"Hi." Elijah smiled as he opened the door.

"Hi." A wide grin crossed my lips as he stood there in a pair of khaki pants and a black button-down shirt.

"Come on in."

I stepped into the foyer and my jaw dropped at the view that was in front of me. The ceilings were at least eleven feet high. There were floor-to-ceiling windows with the most amazing skyline views of the city and wide walnut plank flooring throughout.

"Wow, Elijah. This place is beautiful."

"Thanks. I'll give you the tour after we eat. Dinner is almost ready."

I followed him to the kitchen. A kitchen made up of walnut cabinets with champagne glass panels and beautiful marble countertops that included a cooktop, two ovens, two dishwashers, a built-in coffee station, bar and baking station.

"Did a chef live here before you?" I asked.

"Yes." He grinned. "Can you tell?"

"I can. Lucas would die if he saw this. His second passion is cooking. He comes from a family of chefs."

"Bring him by one night."

I gave him a smile and asked if there was anything I could help with. I felt stupid just standing there.

"Everything is just about done," he said as he handed me a glass of wine.

"What is that delicious smell?" I smiled as I brought the glass up to my lips.

"Garlic Herbed Tenderloin, roasted red potatoes and asparagus."

"How did you have time to prepare that? We've been in court all day."

"I prepped the tenderloin last night and my cleaning lady put it in the oven for me before she left."

"You have a cleaning lady?" I arched my brow.

"Yes. She comes once a week," he spoke as he opened the oven door and bent over to pull the tenderloin from the oven.

The view from behind was amazing. Not only was this man sexy, successful, a god in the bedroom, and smelled like he stepped off the pages of GQ, he also cooked. My entire body was riddled with excitement. An excitement I needed to contain until after dinner.

CHAPTER 37

spen

    I ended up staying the night at Elijah's and then we spent the entire next day together. We took a walk in Central Park, went to the art museum, did some shopping in Times Square, had dinner and then went back to my apartment where he spent the night. Sunday morning we had coffee and breakfast together, then he left because he had plans with his brothers. It was one of the best weekends of my life and I didn't want it to end.

"I think he's the one," I spoke to Geneva as we stood in her kitchen and baked cookies.

"Say what?" She looked at me. "Did I just hear you right?"

"It's crazy. It's way too soon, but I can't help this feeling I have inside for him. I just spent Friday night with him, all day Saturday, part of the morning and I already miss him."

"I think you're in lust." She smiled.

"I don't think so. I really like him. My heart is happy when I think about him and when I'm with him."

She put the cookies in the oven and turned to me.

"Who are you? The Aspen I know doesn't talk like this about a guy."

"I know." I took a seat at the island and put my head down. "I can't believe it either."

"Listen, Aspen." She reached over the island and grabbed my hands. "I don't want you to get hurt."

"I'm not going to get hurt."

"You told me he's never been in a real relationship and he only has casual companions. Do you think men like that can change? I don't. You're already falling for him. What are you going to do when he can't or won't return your affection?"

The oven timer went off. She let go of my hands and pulled the cookies out of the oven.

"I don't think I have to worry about that."

"Lucas, will you tell her men like Elijah Wolfe do not change?" she said as he walked into the kitchen.

"Well, that depends."

"Thank you, Lucas." I smiled.

"But there is a reason he has never been in a relationship and only wants casual companions. Until he resolves those reasons, he'll most likely continue this pattern of behavior. Has he told you why, Aspen?"

"He just said that he refuses to be tied down to anyone and that the thought of committing himself to someone isn't appealing. He said it causes too much chaos in a person's life."

"You said his father left when he was a young child?"

"Yes."

"And he hasn't seen him since?"

"No. I don't think so."

"Sounds to me like he has some abandonment issues. Just like someone else I know." He smirked.

❧

I was lying in bed working on my closing argument for tomorrow when my phone dinged with a text message from Elijah.

"Hi. What are you doing?"

"Lying in bed working on my closing argument. What are you doing?"

"That sounds sexy. Maybe I should join you."

Instantly, a wide grin crossed my lips.

"Come over."

"I'm already here. Are you going to let me in or leave me standing in the hallway with a hard on?"

I jumped up from the bed and ran to the door. Opening it, Elijah stood there with a smile on his face.

"Get in here." I grabbed his shirt and pulled him inside.

Our lips passionately kissed as he picked me up and carried me to the bedroom.

§&

"Foreman, have you reached a verdict?"

"We have, your Honor."

"What say you?"

"In the case of Kind vs. Marsh and for the charge of intentional infliction of emotional distress, we find in favor of the plaintiff and order the defendant to pay the plaintiff in the sum of two million dollars."

I sat there in shock because we were only asking for one million.

"Thank you." Vivian smiled as she hugged me.

Elijah and I grabbed our briefcases and headed out of the building.

"I'll admit, I didn't think at first you could pull it off." He smirked.

"I know you didn't which made me even more determined to win." I grinned. "I can't believe the jury awarded her two million."

"I know. I was shocked. That just goes to show what an amazing lawyer you are." He winked.

When I got back to my office, I noticed a stack of files sitting on my desk.

"Marie, what are these?"

"Ms. Wolfe wanted me to give those to you. They're your new cases."

I sighed as I fell in my chair and opened the first file.

CHAPTER 38

TWO MONTHS LATER

*E*lijah

I threw my pen across my desk and leaned back in my chair. I didn't sleep well, and I was restless. While Aspen was asleep on my chest last night, she said she loved me. I didn't know if she was dreaming or what, but I froze, and then I quietly left. Now, I would have to deal with the aftermath today and I wasn't looking forward to it. I tried to avoid her as much as I could. I came into the office around six a.m. When Marie arrived for work, I told her I wasn't to be disturbed under any circumstances, even for Aspen.

As I was trying to concentrate on a case, my door opened, and Aspen stood there.

"What's going on?" she asked.

"Not now, Aspen. I'm busy."

She stepped inside and shut the door. I sighed.

"You left in the middle of the night without a word. Why?"

"I couldn't sleep, and I didn't want to keep you up."

"Why couldn't you sleep?"

"I don't know. I just couldn't. If you'll excuse me, I have this case I'm working on and I need to concentrate."

"Yeah. Sure. Dinner tonight?"

"Not tonight. I'm meeting up with my brothers."

"Oh. Okay. I'll talk to you later."

She walked out and shut the door. Pushing the intercom button, I told Marie to come into my office.

"Yes, Elijah?"

"I thought I told you I wasn't to be disturbed."

"I'm sorry but I was in the bathroom. What is going on?"

"Nothing is going on. I'm working on this class action suit and I need to focus with no interruptions."

"Fine. I'll tape a sign to your door then."

I rolled my eyes as she walked out.

&

*A*spen

He was acting strange, and I wasn't surprised. So, I just left him alone. It bummed me I wouldn't see him tonight. We'd spent every night together for the last two months, even when he had plans with his brothers. He'd always come by after. But it sounded like he wouldn't do that tonight.

Colleen and I went to Rudy's after work for a few drinks. I hadn't talked to Elijah the rest of the day since I went into his office. Not even a text message. The feeling I expected crept inside me. A feeling I couldn't shake. I'd sent him a text message later that night. No response.

The next morning, as I was preparing for a deposition, Colleen walked into my office and set a report on my desk.

"Is Elijah in yet?"

"Yeah. He's been here for a while. You haven't seen him?"

"No."

"Everyone is here for the deposition. They're waiting in the conference room for you."

"Thanks. I'll be down in a minute."

The depositions went well, and as I was heading back to my office, I saw Olivia Jude and Elijah standing outside his office talking. What the hell was she doing here? I made a quick turn and took the long way back to my office to avoid running into them.

"Aspen." Olivia smiled as she poked her head through the door.

"Olivia. Hi." The corners of my mouth curved upward into a fake smile. "What are you doing here?"

"Elijah and I are working on a case together. His client is suing mine."

"I didn't know you were an attorney."

"I am. I work for Kaufmann, Goldberg and Sands." She stepped inside. "Your name is quite the buzz around our firm."

"Mine?" I pointed to myself.

"Yes. Don't be surprised if the partners get in contact with you. I was asking Elijah about you last night."

"Last night?" I cocked my head.

"Yeah. We had dinner."

A sick feeling erupted in the pit of my belly.

"Anyway, I just had to come by and say hi. Maybe we can meet for lunch sometime."

"Sure." I gave her a fake smile.

"Great. I'll call you and we'll set something up."

I sat there in shock. He lied to me about having plans with his brothers. What the fuck was he doing? Did I dare find out? Or leave him alone and let him come to me with more lies?

I still hadn't seen or heard from him all morning, nor did he reply to my text message last night. So I sent him another one.

"Hey, I'm going to the deli for lunch and I was hoping you'd join me."

"Sorry. I can't. I'm staying in for lunch. I have a lot of work to do."

That pissed me off because now I knew he was avoiding me. I got up from my seat and stormed down to his office.

"Okay. What the hell is going on?" I asked as I stepped inside and shut the door.

"I'm busy, Aspen," he spoke without even looking at me.

"You never responded to my text message last night."

"I got home late, and I didn't want to wake you."

"Late from being out with your brothers or late coming home after your date with Olivia Jude?"

That got his attention as he looked up at me.

"Yeah. I know about your dinner. Olivia stopped by my office this morning and told me."

"We needed to discuss a case."

"Right. Your client is suing her client. You lied to me, Elijah. You told me you were going out with your brothers."

"That was the plan until Olivia called and insisted we meet to discuss the case."

"And you couldn't tell me, why?"

"Why would I tell you? It isn't any of your concern what I do."

I swallowed hard as the anger and hurt rose inside me.

"You're right. I apologize for wanting to know the reason you lied to me."

"I didn't lie. Plans changed at the last minute. Just because we spend some time together and have sex regularly doesn't give you the right to know what I'm doing at all times."

"Where is all of this coming from?" I asked in a harsh tone.

"Where is what coming from, Aspen? You're the one who barged in here demanding answers. I'm telling you like it is," he spoke in a harsh voice. "We'll talk about this later. I'm busy."

"We talk about it now or not at all."

"Fine. I think we spend too much time together and it needs to stop," he spoke as he leaned back in his chair.

"Just all of a sudden?"

"Yes."

"Care to explain why?"

"I don't want to lead you on."

"I see. So this is it? No more lunches or dinners? No more walks in Central Park? No more sleepovers?"

"No. None of it. We had a thing and now it's over."

Suddenly, I felt something I hadn't felt in years. My eyes started to fill with tears. Oh my God, no. Not now. Not in front of him.

"Fine. It's over."

I ran to my office and grabbed my purse.

"Going to lunch," I said to Colleen as I flew past her desk and out of the building.

Once my feet hit the streets, I hailed a cab and one immediately pulled up.

"Where to?" the cab driver asked.

"124 West 79th Street."

CHAPTER 39

*a*spen

My eyes were still filled with tears as I paid the driver and climbed out of the cab. Taking the elevator up to the fifth floor, I opened the door and stepped inside the office.

"Hey, Aspen." Lindsey smiled.

"Is Lucas in there with a patient?"

"No. He's in between patients at the moment."

I opened the door to his office, and he looked up at me from his desk.

"Aspen, what are you—"

The moment he looked at me, I let it all out. The tears I'd been holding back started to stream uncontrollably down my face.

"He doesn't want to see me anymore."

"What? Come here."

He walked over to where I stood and hooked his arm around me and led me to the couch.

"Who? Elijah?"

"Yes. He's been acting weird the past couple of days and then I found out he had dinner with another woman. I confronted him and he said some mean and hurtful things. Then he said we need to stop seeing each other."

He grabbed a tissue from the table and handed it to me.

"Look at me. Look at what's happening. Why is this happening after all these years?"

"Because you truly love him. He hurt you and you're responding in the way most humans do. Did something happen between the two of you for this sudden change in him?"

I hesitated for a moment.

"He left in the middle of the night the other night. When I asked him why, he said he couldn't sleep, and he didn't want to wake me. That's when I noticed the change in him."

"Hmm. You didn't have a fight or an argument of some sort?"

"No. Nothing. Everything was great. We went to bed happy."

"I'm sorry." He kissed the side of my head. "He's obviously dealing with some issues or maybe his feelings for you scared him."

"He said we were spending too much time together, and it needed to stop."

"Ah. Well, I can tell you it sounds like he was getting too close and he freaked out."

We talked for a while longer and then I had to get back to work. I stopped in the bathroom before heading to my office to make sure I looked decent. I didn't want anyone to notice I had been crying.

"How was your lunch?" Colleen smiled.

"It was good. I have a lot of work to do so I don't want to be disturbed. The only person you can disturb me for is Ms. Wolfe."

"Got it. What about Elijah?"

"No. Especially him."

I walked into my office and shut the door.

❧

*E*lijah

It had to be done. Things were getting out of hand, especially for me. The look on her face and the hurt in her eyes was unbearable. Things around here would be difficult for a while, but in time she'd get over it. I knew better, and I should have stayed away like I planned to. I knew she would fall in love, and it was the chance I took just to spend some time with her. She was an amazing woman, and she didn't deserve someone like me. It was better that I broke her heart now than in a few years down the road.

I left the office late and was in no mood to talk to anyone. I walked past Aspen's office and her light was off. She had already left for the night. The moment I stepped into my penthouse, I could still smell the lingering scent of her perfume. Maybe it was just my imagination. My phone rang and Nathan was calling. I sent it to voicemail. He called again. I sent it to voicemail. Suddenly, a text message came through.

"Stop being a dickwad. I know you're home. I'm coming up."

I sighed as I went over to the bar and poured two drinks. The elevator doors opened, and my brother stepped out and walked into the living room. I handed him his drink.

"I'm here because of Mom. She said you were acting like a tyrant today and she sent me here to find out what's going on. So spill."

"I told Aspen that I didn't want to see her anymore."

"Okay. Why did you do that?"

"Because things were getting complicated. And she said in her sleep that she loved me."

"I see the day has come. It's a little sooner than I thought it would, but I knew it was coming. You want to know what I think?"

"No. Actually I don't."

"Well, I'm telling you, anyway. I think you love her too and I don't blame you for being a dick because I would be too. But I see the two of you together. When I look at my playboy style future, I see you both in it. I see you in a big townhome with a couple of kids and a nanny. Maybe a dog or two to complete the perfect family."

"You're fucking crazy."

"Maybe I am or maybe I'm not." He brought his glass up to his lips. "Now, let me tell you what I don't see. I don't see you walking out like Dad did."

"It's over, Nathan."

"Suit yourself. I like Aspen a lot. She's good for you, bro. I've only known her for a couple of months, but I feel like I've known her forever. Mason said the same thing. And you know Mom loves her."

"It doesn't matter what you all think. I said it's over."

"And what am I supposed to tell Mom when she asks me what's going on?"

"You tell her that I told you the same thing I told her. I'm just stressed out about this class action suit. Nothing more. Got it."

"You know I'll always have your back."

I changed the subject, and we bullshitted about sports and other things. After he left, I went to bed. I needed to sleep off this day.

CHAPTER 40

*a*spen

I woke up with a hangover. After I left the office, I went to Geneva's apartment, and we talked, danced and drank until midnight. I felt used by Elijah, but it was partly my fault. I let him. I knew full well what he was like. He held nothing back about relationships. I was stupid to let the defenses down that I'd kept up and held on tightly to since my mother left all those years ago. But as much as I blamed myself for getting hurt, it didn't make me feel any better.

The moment I stepped into my office, Colleen informed me there was a staff meeting.

"I thought the meeting was tomorrow."

"Ms. Wolfe had to reschedule. She has something else going on."

"Great." I rolled my eyes.

I set my things down and headed to the conference room. When I walked in, Elijah looked directly at me. I ignored him and took my seat.

"How is the Crumple case coming along?" she asked me.

"I'm hoping to settle today. If not, we'll be going to court."

"We had a case come in yesterday. One that I want you and Elijah to handle."

"No," Elijah abruptly spoke.

"Excuse me?" She turned to him.

"I'm already over my limit with cases. Especially with this class action suit. Get someone else."

She glared at him for a moment and then turned to me. I immediately looked down.

"Okay. Shannon, you'll be working with Aspen."

When the meeting was over, I grabbed my notepad and went back to my office. I couldn't get far enough away from that asshole.

While I was sitting there staring at Fantasia, Elijah walked in.

"Hey, I just want you to know that when I said no, it wasn't because I didn't want to work with you. It's just I'm a little overloaded right now."

"And I really don't give a fuck what you did or didn't mean." I smiled. "Now leave. I'm busy."

"Listen, Aspen. I'm still your boss."

"How unfortunate for me." I pouted.

He stood there and slowly shook his head before walking out.

Two Weeks Later

Over the past couple of weeks, Elijah and I had very little contact. He only spoke to me when he needed to, and I sat there and listened. I kept myself busy by burying myself in my work. I really didn't have a choice because I was swamped with cases. Thanksgiving was in two weeks, and Geneva and Lucas were going to spend it with his family in Florida. They begged me to come, but I had to decline due to my workload.

"I don't feel right leaving you here on Thanksgiving by yourself. You can fly back earlier than us."

"Geneva, stop worrying about me. I'll be fine."

"Maybe you can have Mom and Raphael over for Thanksgiving?"

"God no. What's wrong with you? Stop! I'll be okay. I promise."

"But it's the first Thanksgiving without Dad."

"I know and again, I'll be fine. I have to go. I have work to do. I'll talk to you later."

I ended the call and got back to work. As I was walking out of my office and looking down at my phone, I ran into Elijah. He lightly grabbed hold of my arm.

"You're not paying attention again," he spoke in a light tone.

"Silly me. Guess I'll never learn," I spoke as I walked away.

The pain in my heart was still there. It hurt every night when I went to bed and it hurt every day when I saw him. Colleen kept pushing me to go out with other guys, but I didn't want to. I was over the man scene for a while.

Day Before Thanksgiving

I had just gotten back from court when I ran into Caitlin in the hallway.

"Oh good. You're back. Can I see you in my office?"

"Sure."

"Have a seat." She smiled. "I had lunch earlier with Bob Kaufmann of Kaufmann, Goldberg & Sands. He was asking a lot of questions about you."

"Why?"

"I think they're interested in bringing you over to their firm. Has anyone of the partners been in contact with you?"

"No. How do they even know me?"

"Word gets around very quickly here in New York. You're happy here, right?"

I wanted to tell her that aside from her asshole son; I was.

"Yes. I am."

"I've noticed some tension lately between you and Elijah. Is everything okay?"

"Everything's fine." I smiled.

"If you weren't happy here, you'd come to me, right?"

"Of course I would. What is this all about?"

"I don't want you to leave my firm. You're a damn good lawyer and I like you." She smiled. "So if there's ever an issue, I want you to come to me and we'll fix it."

"Thank you, Caitlin. I appreciate it."

"Are you spending Thanksgiving with your sister?" she asked.

"No, Geneva and Lucas flew down to Florida to see his parents."

"Oh. What are you doing then?"

"I have a date at home with a fireplace, a warm blanket and a load of case files."

"Absolutely not. You're coming to my house for Thanksgiving."

"Thank you, but no. I can't."

"Yes, you can."

"Caitlin—"

"No arguments. You are not spending your first Thanksgiving in New York alone. Be at my house at two o'clock. I'll text you my address."

What could I do? What could I say? She was my boss and she wouldn't take no for an answer. Ugh. This was going to be a disaster.

"Thank you, Caitlin. You're very kind."

I was packing up for the night and ready to head home when Elijah walked into my office.

"My mother just told me you're coming to Thanksgiving."

"I didn't have a choice. You don't tell the woman who took a chance on you and gave you a job no."

"I'll see you tomorrow." He walked away.

I rolled my eyes and sat back in my chair. Thanks a lot, Geneva.

CHAPTER 41

a spen

I had just gotten out of the bathtub when my phone rang. Picking it up, I saw Elijah was calling. I sighed and declined the call. A second later, he called again. Declined. A moment later a text message came through.

"Pick up your fucking phone! It's important!"

My phone rang again, and I immediately answered it.

"What?"

"I'm on my way to your apartment. Be outside waiting. I got a call from one of our best clients. His son's wife was found murdered. We need to get to the house. I'll be there in less than ten minutes."

"Okay. I'll be waiting."

I threw my phone down on the bed, quickly threw on some clothes, grabbed my purse, and flew down to the lobby. Just as I stepped outside the building doors, a cab pulled up and the door opened. I climbed inside and Elijah gave me a strange look.

"What?"

"Your hair?"

"Shit." I pulled out the tie that held my hair up in a messy bun. "I just got out of the bath. What the hell is going on?"

"Let's address another issue first," he spoke. "The declining of my calls. I am your boss and when I call, you answer."

"I apologize but I didn't think it was about a case. I thought it was a personal call, and I didn't want to talk to you."

"You didn't want to talk to me? Are you serious?"

"Yes. Now what are we dealing with?"

"Brady Marcus is one of our high-end clients and his son, Finn, is being questioned about the murder of his wife."

"Brady Marcus? As in Marcus Fragrances?"

"Yes. Can you please step on it?" he asked the cab driver.

As we stepped into the elevator, Elijah looked at me.

"Have you ever tried a murder case?"

"Yes."

"And?" His brow arched.

"My client was found innocent."

"Good. Have you ever seen a dead body before?"

"No."

"Then you better prepare yourself."

When we reached the penthouse, policemen and investigators filled the space.

"We're the attorneys for Finn Marcus," Elijah spoke to the cop who stopped us at the door. "Where is he?"

"In the kitchen."

Elijah walked ahead of me and I stopped when I saw Mrs. Marcus lying on the floor in a pool of blood.

"Aspen, come on."

We walked into the kitchen to find Mr. Marcus sitting in a chair being questioned by a police officer.

"You're done here. We represent Mr. Marcus and he's not saying another word."

"I didn't do it, Elijah," Finn spoke in a panic.

"Don't say another word, Finn. Not another word."

"What happened here?" I asked the police officer.

"Mrs. Marcus suffered blunt trauma to the head."

"Do you have the weapon used?" I asked.

"Not yet. Your client claims he came home and found her. We need him down at the station for more questioning."

"We'll get him there," Elijah said.

"Mr. Marcus, I'm Aspen Michaelson from Wolfe & Associates. We need to go down to the police station."

"I didn't do it," he spoke in a panicked tone.

"I know. We'll get this figured out. I promise."

The officers found the murder weapon in a dumpster two blocks away.

"Finn Marcus, we are placing you under arrest for the murder of Natalie Marcus."

"What evidence?" I spoke.

"His fingerprints were all over the murder weapon, Miss Michaelson. That's all we need to book him."

"I didn't do it!" Finn exclaimed.

Elijah and I walked out of the room and met with District Attorney Tommy McNeil.

"Elijah," he nodded.

"Tommy. This is Aspen Michaelson. She works at our firm."

"Ah yes." He smiled as he extended his hand. "I've heard a lot about you."

I gave him a confused look as I placed my hand in his.

"It's nice to meet you."

"We're charging your client with first degree murder and asking for life without parole."

"Oh, come on, Tommy," Elijah spoke. "He has no priors, and he has a squeaky-clean record. He said he didn't do it."

"They all say that, Elijah."

"We're filing for an emergency hearing."

"Good luck getting a judge this late." He smirked. "By the way, we're asking for no bail." He walked away.

"That dick." Elijah shook his head.

"How has he heard about me?" I asked.

"Probably from my mother. She's sleeping with him."

"Oh." I furrowed my brows. "I'll be right back."

I stepped off to the side where it was quiet, pulled out my phone and made a call.

"What are you doing?" Elijah asked as he walked up behind me.

"Judge Bloom will be in court in fifteen minutes." I smiled.

"Well done, Miss Michaelson." The corners of his mouth slightly curved upward.

CHAPTER 42

*E*lijah

"Your Honor, Mr. Marcus has no priors, and he isn't a flight risk," I spoke.

"He's a very rich man who comes from a very influential family. He can hop on a plane and flee the country whenever he wants," Mr. McNeil spoke.

"Mr. Marcus, are you going to flee the country?" Judge Bloom asked.

"No, your Honor."

"Your Honor, just because he says—"

"Bail set at one million dollars. Court is adjourned. Can we all go home now?"

Aspen and I climbed into a cab and I had the driver drop her off first.

"At least Finn can spend Thanksgiving with his family," she spoke.

"Speaking of family. Where is yours?"

"My mom is in California, and Geneva and Lucas went to Florida to be with his family. They asked me to go, but I said no."

"Why?"

"I don't know. I really didn't want to travel. Plus, it's the first Thanksgiving without my dad."

"So you'd rather be alone?"

"Yeah. Pretty much."

"Well, that's not happening thanks to my mother."

"No. I guess not." She softly smiled.

The cab pulled up to her building, and she climbed out.

"I'll see you tomorrow," she spoke.

"Thanks for tonight. You did good."

"No problem." She shut the door and walked inside.

That was the most we talked in weeks. I missed her and our conversations. Maybe a little too much.

❧

*W*hen I arrived at my mother's house, Nathan and Mason were already there.

"Happy Thanksgiving, bro." Mason & Nathan both hugged me.

"Happy Thanksgiving."

"There you are." My mother smiled. "Happy Thanksgiving, Elijah."

"Thanks, Mom. Happy Thanksgiving."

"You boys go get a drink while I finish up in the kitchen."

Just as I walked over to the bar, the doorbell rang, and Nathan answered it.

"Aspen. Happy Thanksgiving." He hugged her.

"Hey, Aspen. Happy Thanksgiving." Mason smiled as he took what looked like a pie she was holding and set it in the kitchen.

She took off her coat and looked as beautiful as always.

"Elijah's making some drinks. Come in here," Nathan spoke.

I poured her a scotch and handed it to her.

"Happy Thanksgiving." I smiled.

"Happy Thanksgiving. Thank you."

The doorbell rang again, so I walked over to the door and stood there in shock at who was standing there.

"Happy Thanksgiving, Elijah." Tommy McNeil smiled.

"Happy Thanksgiving. Come in."

"Tommy." My mother grinned as she walked into the foyer and he kissed her cheek.

I walked over to where my brothers and Aspen stood.

"Well, this is awkward." Aspen glanced at me.

"Very." I sighed.

"I didn't know they were that serious." Nathan said.

"He's just another toy for Mom to play with. It won't last."

"I see the apple doesn't fall far from the tree," Aspen spoke and walked away.

"BURN!" Nathan laughed. "Damn, she's good."

"Shut up." I shook my head as I walked away and went into the kitchen.

"Now, I know all about the Marcus case and I want nothing discussed here today. Understand?" My mother said as she looked at the three of us. "The three of you save it for the courtroom."

We all took our seats and enjoyed a great dinner.

"Time for dessert." My mother smiled. "Aspen was kind enough to bring this delicious looking apple pie. We also have pumpkin and cherry. Apple is Elijah's favorite, pumpkin is Nathan's and cherry is Mason's."

"I'll have the apple pie." I smiled as I looked at Aspen and she narrowed her eye at me. "Wow. This is fantastic. Where did you buy it?" I asked her.

"I didn't." She smirked.

"I'm impressed."

"Lucas made it."

"And for a second there I thought you did."

"I would never make an apple pie for you." She smiled.

After dessert, Tommy helped my mother clean up while she told us all to go into the media room. Aspen tried to help but my mother wasn't having it.

"Let's play some cards," Nathan said. "Aspen, do you know how to play poker?"

"I do." She smiled.

"Good. Let me see if I can find them."

He walked over to the cabinets where the wet bar was and started opening them, digging around for a deck of cards.

"Hey. What's this?" He pulled a picture frame out of the cabinet. "It's Mom and some guy. Man, look at how young she was."

Mason and I walked over to where he stood, and I looked at the picture. I had my suspicions of who it was as I quickly grabbed it out of Nathan's hands.

"That's my father," Aspen spoke as she stood behind me. "Why is my father with your mother?"

"Shit," Nathan said.

"All right everyone, time for a game." My mother said as walked into the room.

She froze when she saw all of us staring at her. Aspen took the picture from my hands and walked over to my mother.

"Why are you with my father, Caitlin?"

"Sweetheart," she spoke in a mere whisper as she gave her a sympathetic look.

"It was you, wasn't it? You were the woman my father always talked about. You were the one who broke his heart."

"Yes." My mother looked down. "I'm so sorry, Aspen. We should talk."

"Thank you for dinner. I have to leave now."

She grabbed her coat and walked out of the house.

"Damn it." I looked at my mother.

Grabbing my coat, I ran after her.

CHAPTER 43

*A*spen
I walked down the street as the light snow fell from the sky. I couldn't believe what I saw, and I couldn't believe Caitlin Wolfe was the woman who broke my father's heart.

"Aspen!" I heard Elijah call my name.

"Leave me alone, Elijah."

"Aspen, stop." He lightly took hold of my arm. "Talk to me."

Instantly, I stopped and turned to him.

"Talk to you? We've barely spoken in weeks, and now you want to talk? You don't get that right."

I continued walking and then abruptly stopped again.

"Did you know? Did you?" I shouted.

"She told me a while ago. I didn't know if I should tell you or not. I didn't want to upset you."

"What the fuck, Elijah! You should have told me. But then again, I'm not surprised."

I continued walking.

"What the fuck does that mean?"

"Just leave me alone!"

"Where are you walking to?"

"I don't know!" I shouted.

After walking another block, I stumbled across a bar, so I went inside and took a seat on the stool.

"Happy Thanksgiving. What can I get you?" the bartender asked.

"A bourbon please. And make it a double."

"Coming right up."

As the bartender set down my drink, Elijah sat down on the stool next to me. He ordered a scotch but didn't say a word. He just sat there next to me in silence.

"He was so happy during that time," I spoke. "The happiest I'd ever seen him. He told us he was excited for us to meet someone that was special to him and he had hoped it would be soon. Then one day, I remember him sitting in his room crying. I asked him what was wrong, and he told me that the person who was very special to him decided that they shouldn't see each other anymore. I was only ten at the time and I didn't really understand. But the one thing I under-stood was how hurt my father was. After that, he buried himself in his work to try to forget about her. But he never did. And as the years passed, he would still talk about the woman he had fallen madly in love with."

I turned and looked at Elijah.

"Now it all makes sense."

"What does?" he asked.

"Why I am the way I am. The only thing I've ever seen was broken relationships, hurt and pain. That's why I purposely sabotage all my relationships. Because when it gets too comfortable, I want to prove that things never last. Just like when I told you I loved you." A tear fell from my eye.

I grabbed some cash from my purse, threw it on the bar and walked out. I hailed a cab, and when I climbed in, Elijah flew out the door of the bar. As the cab pulled away from the curb, I stared at him as he stared back with a look of shock across his face.

I headed to the firm. I had work to do, and it was the best way for me to get my mind off everything that was happening. When I walked into my office, I took a seat at my desk and looked at Fantasia, who was lying still at the bottom of her small tank.

"Fantasia?" I tapped the glass. "Fantasia!" I kept tapping.

She didn't move, adding to the misery I already felt.

"I'm so sorry, girl."

"Aspen?"

I looked up and saw Elijah standing in the doorway.

"What's wrong with Fantasia?" he asked.

"She's dead."

"I'm sorry."

"Me too. I have to give her a funeral."

I grabbed the small net, scooped her out, and walked out of my office.

"Are you coming to the funeral?" I asked Elijah.

"Umm. Sure."

He followed me into the bathroom, and I took Fantasia into a stall. Elijah stood next to me.

"You were a great fish and a good friend. You had such a great personality and I'll miss our little talks. Farewell, my friend. May you find peace and swim freely with all the other fishes who have passed on."

I held the net close to the toilet bowl and turned it upside down as she plopped into the water. Looking at Elijah, I gestured that he be the one to flush her down.

"Me? You want me to do it?"

"Yes. You never liked her anyway."

"That is not true, Aspen. She was—pretty."

And just like that she was gone. I sighed as I rinsed the net and went back into my office.

"I know this might not be the best time, but we need to talk."

"I have work to do, Elijah, and can't you see that I'm mourning the death of Fantasia?"

"It's Thanksgiving. You are not working on Thanksgiving, and again, I'm sorry about your fish."

"We have a client who's being charged with first degree murder. I have things to figure out."

"And we will tomorrow," he spoke. "You knew that you told me you loved me? I thought you were talking in your sleep."

"No. I said it fully awake because it was time to see how you really felt about me. And now I know. Mission accomplished. The moment I spoke those three little words, you ran out as fast as you could. Then you avoided me and had dinner the next night with another woman after turning down my dinner invitation."

"I'll tell you for the last time. It was a last-minute thing. It wasn't planned. I didn't call her to have dinner. She called me to discuss a settlement for her client."

"Did you sleep with her?"

"No. Of course not. She tried, and I rejected her. I can't fucking believe you set me up like that. Who does that?"

"A woman who sabotages relationships out of fear. And you're a man who runs away because of his fear. We are just two people bound by fear who have no business being together."

"God. I can't even look at you right now," he spoke with irritation.

"Then go. Nobody's stopping you. Why did you even come looking for me?"

"Because you're upset."

"So? You didn't seem to care how upset I was when you told me you were done with me."

"Aspen, don't."

"Don't what? Tell the truth? Isn't that what we as adults are supposed to do? Just tell me the fucking truth!"

"Yeah. I cared that I upset you, but there was nothing I could do about it. I had to end it after you told me you loved me. And I think that's exactly what you wanted." He pointed at me.

"You're crazy." I laughed.

"No. Actually, I'm not. You knew exactly how I felt about women falling in love with me. You knew how I felt about relationships and yet you still said it knowing how I felt. You were just as freaked out about what we had as I was and that was your way of getting out without looking like the bad guy."

"I cried over you!" I pointed at the ground. "For the first time in years, tears fell from my eyes that day!"

"But you didn't plan on that happening. Did you? That caught you off guard."

"Maybe. I was so hurt and angry and I didn't expect to feel that bad. I mean, I knew I would be upset for a while because I really liked you, but it still hurts so much, and I hate that I can't get over us."

He walked over to me and placed his hands on each side of my face.

"I miss you, Aspen, and I'm not afraid to tell you. I hate that I can't get over us either."

"I miss you, too."

"So now what?" he asked. "What do two people who are bound by fear do?"

I turned away from him and sighed.

"I don't know, Elijah. We're both fucked up."

"That's true." He chuckled. "We're two fucked up people who both come from broken families with issues we never dealt with. But maybe we can be fucked up together and heal each other one day at a time"

"Are you asking me to get into a relationship with you?"

"Let's not be hasty." He put his hand up. "Maybe we can spend some time together and see what happens. As long as we're in an agreement that if either of us begins to freak out or fear consumes us, we'll talk about it." He smiled.

"I guess we can try it and see." I softly smiled.

"How about I walk you home?" He held out his arm.

"I think that would be okay." I put on my coat, my knit hat, and grabbed my purse.

I placed my arm around his and we walked out of the building together.

"I suppose you'll want sex when we get back to my place," I said as we walked down the street in the lightly falling snow.

"You're the one who brought it up." He kissed the side of my head. "If you want to, I won't object, and I'll be more than happy to accommodate your needs."

"I have one rule or else it isn't going to happen."

"And what rule is that?" He smiled.

"You have to dance with me when we get back to my place."

"Slow dance?" His eye narrowed at me.

"No." I grinned.

"If I don't dance with you, you won't have sex with me? Is that what you're saying?"

"Yes."

"I'll think about it." He winked.

CHAPTER 44

ONE MONTH LATER

Elijah

"We the jury, find the defendant on the charge of first-degree murder, not guilty."

I let out the biggest sigh of my life as I shook Finn's hand.

"Thank you, Elijah. Thank you, Aspen. Thank you so much."

"We make a pretty good team." I smiled at Aspen as we headed back to the office.

"We do. Don't we?"

Things between us were really good. In fact, they were great. Aspen and my mother had a long talk which made me nervous, but it all worked out. They talked about Aspen's father and my mother told her things she never knew. They were growing close and as much as it made me happy to see, it also kind of freaked me out.

I wouldn't lie and say that my fears went away, because they didn't. Just like Aspen's didn't either. We both were casually seeing each other with no expectations. We met Geneva and Lucas once a week for dinner, and she was now a part of our family dinners per my mother's request.

I did something after Thanksgiving I thought I'd never do. I went out and bought her a new fish for her desk. She was grateful, but now

I had to say good morning to the damn thing every day when I walked into her office. I didn't mind though. I was just happy to make her happy.

❧

Christmas Day

I softly stroked her arm as I stared at her while she slept. A soft smile crossed her lips as she opened her eyes.

"Merry Christmas." I smiled as I softly brushed my lips against hers.

"Merry Christmas. What a beautiful way to wake up." She brought her hand up to my face.

"I'll go make us some coffee and then we can open presents."

"I love that idea." She grinned.

As we both climbed out of bed, I pulled on my pajama bottoms and she slipped into her soft pink silk robe. I made us each a cup of coffee and we sat down by the tree. She made me open all my gifts first, and I loved every one of them. Especially the rare edition of a law book I'd always wanted.

"How did you find this? I've been searching for months?"

"I have my secrets, Mr. Wolfe."

I smiled as I kissed her lips.

"Your turn."

I handed her the first gift. A new coat she'd been eyeing for the past month. The second gift I gave her was a pair of Jimmy Choo boots she'd also been eyeing but wouldn't buy for herself. After many hugs and kisses, I told her I'd be right back. I went into the bedroom, opened the drawer, and pulled out a small box wrapped in a gold foil paper.

"I have one more for you." I handed her the box.

She took the box with a smile and delicately removed the ribbon and then the paper. Lifting the lid, her eyes lit up when she saw the white gold and sapphire ring encased with diamonds.

"Elijah, this is so beautiful."

"It's a promise ring, Aspen. I think we should make our companionship official."

"As in an official couple? The two of us together as a couple? A boyfriend and girlfriend type couple?"

"Yes." I swallowed hard. "I believe that's what we already are. But I'm making it official now. That's if you'll accept."

"Doesn't this scare the shit out of you?" she asked.

"Well, yes, a little. I've never done this before, and I'm scared I won't be any good at it."

A wide grin crossed her face.

"You're already perfect at it." She kissed my lips. "And yes, I will officially be your girlfriend."

I took the ring out of the box and slipped it on her right ring finger.

"You're not going to try to sabotage this, are you?" I narrowed my eye at her.

"Nah. I'm too in love with you, Elijah Wolfe."

I brought my hand up to her face and softly stroked her cheek while I stared in her eyes.

"I love you too, Aspen Michaelson."

CHAPTER 45

ONE YEAR LATER

*A*spen

Elijah and I took it one step further and moved in together about three months after Christmas. I gave up my apartment and moved into his penthouse. I was happy. We were happy, and our relationship was perfect, even though we liked to argue. But we were lawyers, and that's what we did. It was all in fun.

"What's going on?" Elijah asked as he stepped off the elevator.

"I'm freaking out and I'm letting you know."

"Okay. What are you freaking out about?"

"Well, I haven't had a period in two months."

"Oh. Did you go to the doctor?" He nervously asked.

"Nope. I took a trip to the drugstore and bought this." I held up the box that contained a pregnancy test.

"Oh. Now *I'm* freaking out."

"Good. I was hoping you would be. Here's how this will work. I'll go into the bathroom, pee on the stick, and then we'll wait and read the results together."

"Okay. Let's do it." He held his hand out to me.

I grabbed his hand, led him upstairs and brought him in the bathroom with me.

"How would this have happened?" he asked as I held the stick under the stream of urine.

"We were reckless. Remember when I switched birth control pills, and I told you we should use condoms just to be safe and you said no we're fine?" I smiled.

"Yes. I remember." He sighed.

I set the stick on the counter and as I started to set the timer, Elijah stopped me.

"There's no need to set the timer. Look. Yep. You're definitely pregnant. See, it says it right there." He pointed to the word.

"Okay then." I took in a deep breath. "I guess we're having a baby."

"I guess we are," he said as he stared into my eyes.

"I'm not going to lie. I'm scared, Elijah."

"Me too, sweetheart." He wrapped his arms around me and held me tight. "But, as scared as we are, we can do this." He kissed my forehead.

"Right?" I broke our embrace. "We are two professional lawyers who win a shitload of cases. Hard cases. There isn't anything we can't do. Pfft." I waved my hand. "We can do this parenting thing."

"We sure can. Raising a baby will be a piece of cake compared to the work we do."

"Exactly. We got this."

"Yeah. We got this." He smiled as he pulled me back into an embrace.

§•

*A*fter getting confirmation from my doctor, we went to family dinner where we would make the big announcement to Elijah's family. We had already told Geneva and Lucas a few days before and they were both over the moon, even though they didn't plan on having children. Hell, I didn't plan on it either, but here we were.

We took our seats at the table. Elijah and I discussed our plan beforehand and decided it was better to spring the news on them while we ate, hoping that no one would choke on their food when we told them.

"We have something to tell you," Elijah said.

Caitlin, Nathan and Mason stopped eating and stared at us.

"Oh, my gosh. You two are getting married!" Caitlin exclaimed. "It's about time. Have you set the date yet? We'll have the engagement party here at the house."

"Mom. Stop. We're not getting married."

Nathan started laughing. "Then what? Are you two having a kid or something?"

"Yes. We're having a baby," Elijah spoke.

Nathan dropped his fork and Mason spit out the water he was just sipping.

"What?" Caitlin asked as she cocked her head.

"We're having a baby." I smiled.

She placed her hand over her mouth, got up from her chair, and gave each of us a hug.

"I'm going to be a grandmother?"

"Yes, Mom, you're going to be a grandmother."

"Grandma Caitlin. I love it." Mason laughed.

"Wow. Congrats to both of you." Nathan smiled. "We're going to be uncles." He glanced at Mason.

"Congrats you two." Mason held up his glass.

CHAPTER 46

SEVEN MONTHS LATER

*A*spen

Elijah and I felt very prepared for the arrival of our daughter. We had read every book out there, got the nursery ready and took Lamaze classes. Yep. That's right. WE. WERE. READY. I was over this pregnancy. I was huge, my feet were swollen, my back hurt and I couldn't sleep. I had two weeks left and I couldn't wait for this child to be born. Uncomfortable was an understatement.

"I'm hungry," I said as we lay in bed, both of us on our laptops working.

"You just ate an hour ago."

I slowly turned my head and narrowed my eye at him.

"I'm sorry. Let me rephrase that. Your daughter is hungry!"

"And what would my daughter like to eat?"

"Do we have any of that chocolate chip ice cream left?"

"No. You finished it off last night."

"What about those brownies Lucas made?"

"Nope. You finished those off too."

"Ugh. Well, I need something sweet and sugary!"

He gave me a smile as he reached under the bed and pulled out a big box of Godiva Chocolates.

"Where did you get that?!" I asked with excitement.

"I picked it up today on the way home. Somehow I knew you'd be wanting something sweet and sugary and you've already eaten everything else in the house."

"Have I told you how much I love you?" I smiled as I kissed his lips.

"Tell me again."

"I love you."

"And I love you just as much. Now open that box and dig in."

I untied the ribbon and slowly lifted the lid in anticipation of the mouthwatering chocolates that sat inside. When I removed the top of the box, I gasped when I saw the most beautiful diamond ring I had ever seen sitting in the middle amongst the luxurious chocolates. I look over at Elijah as he took the ring out of the box and held it up.

"I love you, Aspen. You have gone from being my companion to my girlfriend and now the mother of my child. I would do anything in this world to have you as my wife. Will you marry me?"

"Doesn't this scare the hell out of you?" I asked.

"No. Actually it doesn't." He smiled.

"In that case, yes, Elijah. I will marry you! I can't believe this! I planted him with a thousand kisses. "I love you so much."

"I love you too, sweetheart, and I can't wait for you to become Mrs. Elijah Wolfe."

❧

One Week Later

"Five hundred thousand dollars and not a penny less."

"No way, Miss Michaelson," Mr. Adams spoke.

I sat in the conference room with my hand on my belly, trying to conceal the fact that I was in massive pain.

"Mr. Adams." I stopped for a moment and began taking in long deep breaths. In and out.

"Miss Michaelson, are you okay?"

"I'm fine. Your client denied my client the promotion he promised her and then fired her because she wouldn't sleep with him. OH GOD!"

"He fired your client because of poor performance. Are you sure you're okay?"

"Are you referring to work performance or sexual performance?"

"I object, Miss Michaelson."

I stood up, gripped the edge of the table and looked over at Rhonda, the court reporter.

"My water just broke. Can you please go get Mr. Wolfe?"

Elijah came running into the conference room.

"What's wrong, sweetheart?"

"My water broke and I'm in labor."

"Come on. Let's get you to the hospital," he said as he lightly grabbed my arm.

"No. I'm not going anywhere until we settle this."

"Aspen—"

"Shut up, Elijah. Five hundred thousand dollars or we go to trial where I will air all of Mr. Peterson's dirty little secrets. OH GOD!" I leaned over the table.

"What dirty little secrets are you referring to?"

"His gambling addiction. His frequent visits to strip clubs. His late-night meetings with a certain call girl, and a signed affidavit from a former employee who was a witness to Mr. Peterson's sexual misconduct towards other female employees."

"You're bluffing. My client is an upstanding citizen of this community. Not only does he go to church every Sunday, he has donated millions of dollars to children's charities. He is a real respected businessman."

"What a saint. Holy shit!" I took in a deep breath.

"Aspen. We have to go," Elijah said.

I slid a legal-sized envelope across the table to Mr. Adams. He opened it, took out the contents and then looked at me.

"A jury will probably award more after seeing those photos. We'll just take this to court. Thank you for your time. Now if you'll excuse me, I need to go have this baby."

Elijah hooked his arm around me and led me to the door.

"Miss Michaelson?"

"Yes, Mr. Adams?" I turned and looked at him.

"Four hundred thousand dollars and that's our final offer."

"Deal. I'll let my client know the case is settled. Have a good day, Mr. Adams."

Elijah held onto me as he walked me out of the building.

"Good job in there." He kissed the side of my head. "You would have taken three hundred thousand, wouldn't you?"

"Yes." I smiled as I continued my breathing.

CHAPTER 47

SIX MONTHS LATER

*E*lijah

Life was crazy, but a good crazy. I had two amazing girls in my life. My soon to be wife and my daughter, Mila Rose. I never thought it was possible to love two people so much. In the span of two years, my life had completely done a 180. I went from being a man who only cared about work and using women for my own needs, to becoming a man whose family was first and foremost a priority. Nothing in this world was more important to me than Aspen and my baby girl.

"I have to admit, bro, this is kind of weird," Nathan said. "I never thought I'd be walking down the street with you pushing a baby stroller."

"Yeah. It feels weird," Mason spoke.

"Thanks for coming along. Our nanny has the flu and Aspen is in court all day."

"Check it out." Mason hit Nathan's arm. "Check out the women that keep staring at us as they walk by."

"Women always check us out, bro. Nothing new."

"No. This is different. I think it's because of the kid."

"Give me the stroller, Elijah," Nathan spoke as he pushed me out of the way.

"Oh, my gosh. What an adorable little girl." An attractive young woman stopped us.

"Thank you." Nathan grinned.

"I bet you're an awesome Daddy. I could just eat you up," she said as she bent down and looked at Mila.

"I'd love to take you up on that offer." He smiled, and I smacked him.

"The child is mine, not his, and we really need to get going," I said as I grabbed the stroller from Nathan.

"Oh. Well, she is adorable."

She walked away and Nathan shot me a look.

"Thanks a lot, bro."

"What the hell is wrong with you? Wait until I tell Aspen that you're using our kid to pick up women."

"You make it sound like it's a bad thing. Can I borrow her sometime?"

"No, you cannot! Go have your own kid."

"I'm sure there's a little Wolfe running around somewhere in the world." Mason laughed.

"Hilarious, dickwad."

⸱⸱⸱

I arrived home and put Mila down for her nap. Just as I sat down to relax, Aspen stepped off the elevator.

"You're home early." I smiled as I held out my arms.

"I came right from court. I missed you and Mila." She sat on my lap and kissed my lips.

"We missed you too."

"How was your day with her?"

"It was good. We ran some errands and went to Central Park for a while. Nathan and Mason were trying to use our daughter to pick up women."

"I'm not surprised." She laughed. "Is she sleeping?"

"Yes. I just put her down for a nap."

"Good." She started to unbutton my shirt. "Then we have some alone time and I think we better take advantage of it."

"I love the way you think, counsel," I spoke as I passionately kissed her.

Stayed tuned for more of the Wolfe brothers releasing in 2020.
Nathan Wolfe
Mason Wolfe

THE EXCEPTION

CHAPTER 1

*J*illian

I could hear the soft music play as the guests started to gather inside the church and took their seats in the wooden pews that were beautifully decorated with white satin bows and white roses. My mother and my bridesmaids were shuffling around, making sure that everything was to perfection, including me.

"Giorgio, darling. Come here and fix Jillian's eye shadow," my mother ordered as she snapped her fingers.

"Of course, of course," he spoke as he came running over to me.

"My eyeshadow is fine, Giorgio. Please step away from me before I lose my shit." I casually smiled.

His eyes widened as he set down his shadow palette and slowly walked away. I took in a deep breath as I stared at myself in the full-length mirror, dressed in white from head to toe, in a wedding dress that I hated. A dress my mother picked out. This day had been planned since I was born and I should be happy, right? After all, it was my wedding day. The day every girl dreamed of.

The girl staring back at me was someone I didn't recognize. I didn't know her. Everyone who had ever known me knew her. But to me, she was a stranger. As everyone was hustling and bustling around,

I slipped out the side door of the room and made my way down the hall, where I looked out into the church and saw Grant standing at the altar with his best man, Paris. I was numb. Completely numb with no feeling inside me. When I looked down at my engagement ring, it had no meaning. As I removed it from my finger, I looked around and saw the side exit door of the church. This was my chance. It was now or never. I slipped back inside the dressing room.

"There you are, darling. It's time to line up. The ceremony is about to begin."

"I'll be out in a minute, Mom. I just want to be alone for a few minutes to calm my nerves."

"Now, Jillian dear, there's nothing to be nervous about. You've waited your whole life for this day."

I flashed her my fake smile. A smile that I had perfected over the years.

"I know. I just need a few moments. Okay?"

"Okay. We'll be outside the door waiting for you."

As soon as everyone left, I grabbed my purse, took my phone out, and dialed a cab to pick me up at Pier 59. After doing a factory reset on my phone, I threw it down on the chair and laid my ring next to it. Turning around, I took one last look at the stranger in the mirror. Ripping the veil off my head, I quietly slipped out the other door and left the church without anyone noticing me. Nerves flooded throughout my body as I ran to the limo, climbed inside, and told the driver to step on it.

Pulling up to Pier 59, I climbed out of the limo and straight into the cab.

"Where to, lady?" the driver asked as he gave me a strange look.

"The Travelodge on 6th Avenue. And I'll need you to wait for me because I'm going to the airport."

"Sure. Okay."

As soon as he pulled up to the hotel, I told him that I'd be a few minutes and took the elevator to the second floor. Inserting the key card into the lock, I stepped inside the room and stripped out of my wedding dress. Unzipping the suitcase that was lying on the bed, I changed into a black maxi dress, slipped my feet into my black flip-flops, unpinned my brown hair, threw it up in a ponytail, and grabbed my other purse, which had my wallet and new phone in it. I took my luggage down to the lobby, handed it to the cab driver and climbed inside.

The reality of what I'd done finally set in and tears began to stream down my face. The emptiness I'd felt inside me for so long was still there, even though I was free. Free from the rope that my parents had tied around my neck since the day I was born. My mind was cluttered with chaos and racing a mile a minute, and the perfect wedding that was twenty-four years in the making was ruined. It wasn't my fault. How could I marry someone I didn't love? I could no longer pretend to be the happy perfect Jillian Bell everyone believed I was. A weight had been lifted off my shoulders and a new life was about to emerge. A life that I would be solely responsible for creating.

As I walked through the airport, pulling my carry-on behind me, I realized that I hadn't eaten a single thing all day. My mother had told me that if I ate before the ceremony, I would bloat and that was the only thing the guests would be focusing on. I was starving, so I stopped at La Pisa Café and ordered a panini and a bag of chips. As I was sat down and took a single bite of my panini, I pushed the button on my phone to check the time. *Shit.* My flight was already boarding. Setting my panini down on the plate, I shoved the bag of chips into my purse, grabbed my carry-on, and headed to my gate. When I reached the gate, I noticed it said the flight was going to Houston, Texas. Looking at my boarding pass, I asked the attendant behind the desk where the flight to LAX was.

"That flight was moved to Gate C24."

"Since when?" I asked abruptly.

"About thirty minutes ago." She politely smiled.

"But that's all the way at the other end of the airport and it's boarding now!"

"Then I suggest you run. An announcement was made overhead."

Shaking my head, I started to run through the airport to gate C24. This was my punishment, my karma for leaving Grant at the altar.

Instead of sitting down with him and my parents, I took the coward's way out and ran and I was still running. This was unbelievable. Who does that sort of thing? A person who's been held a prisoner all her life for far too long and snaps. That's who. Just as I made it to the gate, they were getting ready to close the doors.

"WAIT!" I shouted breathlessly as I handed the attendant my boarding pass.

"You're lucky. You made it just in time."

Stepping onto the packed plane, I stopped dead in my tracks when I saw the person who was in the seat next to mine.

"Ah, shit," I silently spoke to myself. This was definitely my punishment. Dark hair, business suit, face of a god punishment.

Taking in a deep breath, I opened the overhead and he looked up at me, his dark brown eyes locked on mine through my sunglasses.

"I don't think there's any room up there."

"I can see that," I spoke as I shut the overhead.

Suddenly, a flight attendant approached me and took my carry-on from my hand.

"I'll find a space for it. Just sit down. We're taking off now."

"Thank you. Can I get a glass of wine, please?"

"As soon as we're up in the air, I'll bring you one." She gently smiled.

The man sitting next to me stood up so I could get to my seat with ease. Removing the pillow and the blanket, I sat down and took in a deep breath.

"Are you a nervous flier?" he asked.

Slowly turning my head, I looked at him through the sunglasses that I was still wearing.

"No."

"Well, just the way you wanted a glass of wine before you even sat down led me to believe you were."

Seriously? What business was it of his if I wanted a glass of wine?

"It's just been a really shitty day," I spoke as I looked out the window.

"I'm sorry to hear that. I hope it gets better for you." He politely smiled and then went back to looking at his phone.

As the plane lifted off the ground, I stared at the life I was leaving behind. A life that was never truly mine to begin with. My heart started racing and my skin became heated. Reaching up, I twisted the knob to the air vent as the rush of cool air poured down on me and I let out a breath.

"I thought you weren't a nervous flier," the man spoke.

"It's not the flight." I laid my head against the window.

CHAPTER 2

*J*illian

"Here you go, miss," the flight attendant spoke as she handed me my wine.

"Thank you."

I didn't waste any time gulping down half the glass. I needed it more than I thought I did. Realizing that I still had my sunglasses on, I removed them and set them in my purse.

"You've been crying," the man who was all too fucking nosey, but seriously hot as fuck, especially with that light stubble across his jaw, spoke.

"How do you know that?" I asked with an attitude.

"Your makeup." He swept his finger under his eye.

Sighing, I took out the compact from my purse and opened it. *Ugh.* He was right. I looked like a raccoon. So much for the waterproof mascara Giorgio put on me. I got up from my seat and went to the bathroom. After cleaning myself up and reapplying my eyeliner and mascara, I sat down in my seat and looked at him.

"Better?" I spoke sarcastically.

He gave me a small but incredible smile. "I didn't think it looked bad before."

Looking down, my heart skipped a beat. This was the last thing I needed; to sit next to a sexy man who was trying to flirt with me just hours after I left my entire life behind and my fiancé standing at the altar.

"So, where are you traveling to?" he asked as I stared out the window.

"Hawaii," I replied.

"Me too. Are you traveling alone?"

"Yeah." I sighed. "Listen, I don't mean to be rude or anything, but I'm really not in a talkative mood."

"I understand. Sorry. After all, you did have a shitty day and I know when I have a shitty day, I'm not in the mood to talk either."

"Good. I'm happy you understand." I sighed.

I signaled for the flight attendant and asked her for another glass of wine. Bringing my knees up, I placed the pillow against the window and leaned my head against it. I was exhausted, both physically and mentally. My mind couldn't help but wonder what was happening back in Seattle. The look on my mother's face when she found I was gone. The embarrassment on Grant's face when I never walked down the aisle. The whispers of the guests who gave up their time to attend a wedding that never happened. A tear ran down my cheek, and not because I was sad about what I'd done. I wasn't entirely sure why the tear fell from my eye. Maybe it was because I wasn't a robot anymore, looking at my life from the outside. I no longer had to pretend to be happy, and every smile that crossed my lips from now on would be real and genuine.

"Here." The man handed me a tissue.

Taking it from him, I wiped my eyes.

"Thanks."

"You're welcome. I wouldn't want your mascara to run again." He smirked.

A smile fell upon my face. A real smile. A smile that made me feel good inside.

"Here's your wine." The flight attendant handed me my glass. "May I get you anything else?"

"Is there a meal service on this flight?"

"No. I'm sorry. Light snacks only, but there will be a meal served on your connecting flight from LAX."

The man reached down in the small bag he had under the seat in front of him and pulled out a protein bar.

"Eat this." He handed it to me.

"Thanks, but no, I'm fine."

"Obviously, you're hungry. Don't you like protein bars?" He smiled.

"I like protein bars. I eat them almost every day. Thank you for the offer, but I can wait."

He shrugged. "Suit yourself. If you're not going to eat it, then I will." He removed the wrapper and took a bite.

"You don't even know me and you're offering me your protein bar. Why?" I asked out of curiosity.

"Because you had a shitty day. It's the least I could do to try and make your day a little better. That way, you can tell everyone that a nice gentleman on the plane gave you his protein bar because you were hungry."

I let out a light laugh and shook my head. God, it felt good to laugh.

"See." He smiled. "I think I just made your day a little less shitty."

I laughed again. "Maybe I'll just have a piece."

He broke the bar in half and handed it to me.

"Thank you—" I cocked my head and narrowed my eye.

"Drew. Drew Westbrook." He stuck out his hand.

"Nice to meet you, Drew. Jillian Bell." I politely placed my hand in his.

"Jillian. That's a beautiful name."

I could feel the heat rise in my cheeks as I thanked him. A heat that I'd never felt before.

"I think I'm going to watch a movie," I spoke as I took the headphones out of the package the flight attendant gave me.

Looking at his watch, Drew spoke. "You won't have enough time. We're landing in about an hour."

"Oh. Okay, then I think I'll just take a nap. Could you please wake me when we land?"

"Of course." He nodded.

⁊

*D*rew

    Jillian Bell. A beautiful name for an incredibly beautiful woman. The minute she stepped onto the plane, I took notice of her. Her brown hair with the subtle blonde highlights pulled back in a ponytail and her five-foot-six small-framed but very toned body that sported the black maxi dress she wore to perfection. I hated that she kept on those damn Gucci sunglasses for so long because I needed to see her eyes. When she finally took them off and I saw the ocean blue staring back at me, I was left breathless, even with the mascara stains underneath them. She was broken, that much I could tell, and there was a part of me that wanted to reach out and fix her. A complete stranger. Something I didn't do. I was curious as to why she was traveling to Hawaii alone. Something happened. A break-up, perhaps? I wanted to know, and I was going to find out more about Jillian Bell before our plane landed in Hawaii.

As she rested her head on the pillow, I couldn't help but stare at her. Even while she attempted to sleep, she didn't seem at peace. I sighed as I looked down at my iPad and sorted through some emails. Every time she stirred, I looked over at her to make sure she was okay.

I hope you enjoyed this preview of The Exception. You can download the book by clicking the link below:

Amazon Universal Link:

getbook.at/TheException

208

BOOKS BY SANDI LYNN

If you haven't already done so, please check out my other books. Escape from reality and into the world of romance. I'll take you on a journey of love, pain, heartache and happily ever afters.

Millionaires:

The Forever Series (Forever Black, Forever You, Forever Us, Being Julia, Collin, A Forever Christmas, A Forever Family)

Love, Lust & A Millionaire (Wyatt Brothers, Book 1)

Love, Lust & Liam (Wyatt Brothers, Book 2)

Lie Next To Me (A Millionaire's Love, Book 1)

When I Lie with You (A Millionaire's Love, Book 2)

Then You Happened (Happened Series, Book 1)

Then We Happened (Happened Series, Book 2)

His Proposed Deal

A Love Called Simon

The Seduction of Alex Parker

Something About Lorelei

One Night In London

The Exception

Corporate A$$

A Beautiful Sight

The Negotiation

Defense

Playing The Millionaire

#Delete

Behind His Lies

Carter Grayson (Redemption Series, Book One)

Chase Calloway (Redemption Series, Book Two)

Jamieson Finn (Redemption Series, Book Three)

Damien Prescott (Redemption Series, Book Four)

The Interview: New York & Los Angeles Part 1

The Interview: New York & Los Angeles Part 2

One Night In Paris

Perfectly You

The Escort

The Ring

Second Chance Love:

Rewind

Remembering You

She Writes Love

Love In Between (Love Series, Book 1)

The Upside of Love (Love Series, Book 2)

Sports:

Lightning

ABOUT THE AUTHOR

Sandi Lynn is a *New York Times, USA Today* and *Wall Street Journal* bestselling author who spends all her days writing. She published her first novel, *Forever Black*, in February 2013 and hasn't stopped writing since. Her mission is to provide readers with romance novels that will whisk them away to another world and from the daily grind of life – one book at a time.

Be a part of my tribe and make sure to sign up for my newsletter so you don't miss a Sandi Lynn book again!

Facebook: www.facebook.com/Sandi.Lynn.Author
Twitter: www.twitter.com/SandilynnWriter
Website: www.sandilynnbooks.com
Pinterest: www.pinterest.com/sandilynnWriter
Instagram: www.instagram.com/sandilynnauthor
Goodreads: http://bit.ly/2w6tN25
Newsletter: http://bit.ly/sandilynnbooks
Bookbub: http://bit.ly/sandilynnbookbub

Printed in Great Britain
by Amazon

44455465R00124